Samantha Dunn

failing Paris

Text copyright ©Samantha Dunn, 1999
All rights reserved.
Printed in the United States of America.

Published by AmazonEncore
P.O. Box 400818
Las Vegas, NV 89140

ISBN-13: 9781612182452
ISBN-10: 1612182453

Failing Paris

For Deanne Harris, Peter Matson,
the women of Hard Words,
the spirit of Donald Rawley
and my blue, blue angels

Monday

Chapter one

This is how it is. It's as if I'm watching you stare at the lines *nom, prenom,* on which have been typed Wilcox, Sabine, fingering the edge of your student card. The room smells stagnant, as if it has never been dry. You are gripping that card because you might not recognize your own name when it's called. That could happen. That really could happen. You could forget that you have come to the Hôpital Saint-Louis to undergo the perfunctory psychological evaluation, the one required by the French government that will allow you to make another appointment for next week, when you can have the abortion. *L'avortement,* which means the failure, the plans which have fallen through.

In the next five minutes or fifteen or even two hours from now (how does time parcel itself, one moment becoming separate from another?), there will come the most difficult French test of your life. There's a chance you will have to argue why you must have this procedure. They will say, How many weeks has it been? and you'll say, I don't know. I never keep track of these things. If the nurses even hint there is some question about you being a deserving candidate, that you waited too long to do it safely, if they say in that way meant to console, What's the worst thing that can happen if you carry to term?, you will give specifics. You could even draw a picture.

In Mesilla, New Mexico, Miss Ortiz has framed the article the *Doña Ana County Courier* published about your scholarship from the Lion's Club, the largest one ever given, probably in the whole state, or at least south of Socorro, since big things happen all the time up north in Santa Fe and Albuquerque. That's the way they would say it. Big things. You were in the parade at the Whole Enchilada Fiesta. People said isn't Bean (because Sabine sounds so fancy) such a good student, she gets to go all the way to France, and isn't it inspiring how she got beyond that tragic situation when the police were called after Nick Navarro took his rifle to the barn? People said, Her mother fell to pieces and just depended on that girl, and other people said, The woman was already broken.

Miss Ortiz has placed the *Courier* piece right next to the blackboard and points to it as the example of what can be accomplished. If the follow-up to that was that you got pregnant, quit school, the article would come down. Not that it would be a shock, how you turned out. It just wouldn't be exceptional. Most would say, look at the odds. How could it be otherwise? She is the daughter of a woman who burns bridges with an arsonist's zeal. You think you carry a mark because of that, have always tried to hide it, but let's admit now that it will never be removed, no matter how many layers you peel from your skin. The saying goes that you shouldn't lead a life of crime and extravagance with a tattooed face, but what choice is there, really?

You know how to study (a series of repetitions, the paths of neurotransmitters) but it has not been explained how they evaluate, what they will weigh, measure, and so there is no way to practise the answers for this test. What you mean to say is, it's been all this time and still you haven't been to the arrondissement where the Eiffel Tower is, but you do know by name the transvestite waiter at the restaurant, Le Mouton Enragé, the Furious Sheep, the one near the cemetery where you pretend to visit dead relatives. You go to the Louvre on Sundays because there is no entrance fee, and you shake at the beauty you find there, though you do not recognize the names of the artists, or the styles of the brush strokes or the forms of the granite. But you take the pamphlets. They're free. You want to learn.

A name is called and you check your card again but you have stared at the lines so long they no longer make sense. Is it you? No. Another woman gets up and moves to the door, her hair dull as a cowbird's wing and chopped unevenly at the back.

The nurse brushes past the others in the waiting-room but hesitates in front of your chair.

—*Ne vous inquiétez pas,* Don't worry, mademoiselle, it is just a formality, the nurse says, and this is a lullaby in her throat.

You look up, startled, and your eyes dart around. Relax. She's talking to you. Smile now, and even start to laugh, the pitch and crack of it high enough to pierce. The nurse regards you oddly and so do the other women in the waiting-room but you continue. Worried. How could you look worried? Finally it has become clear. *Voilà,* the real moment, the moment to which all others have led. The joke was on you, memorizing dead French poets, in your bedroom parroting cassettes of absurd conversations you would never have about the weather and the character of others, *il fait un temps épouvantable; Coco n'était jamais sympatique, elle était toujours un vrai monstre sacré.* This in your house with aluminum siding that doesn't even pretend to be wood grain, with its tears in the screened-in porch, red caliche earth, pecan trees rooted deeply in their rows, the interstate's whining rubber never far off. Why you rode your horse bareback across the pasture to the French teacher's house during school breaks, the old maid with yellow barrettes in her black hair, an *au pair* thirty years ago but she gave you all she knew.

Yet, despite your diligence, when you arrived you were so far out of your element you felt the way drowning must feel, struggling and choking and the flood of what's all around coming in too fast. So to make your way, you used skin like currency across crisp cotton sheets, the attention of men so much easier, the only ones who have anything to gain by talking to foreign girls. It was all in trade for the ease of saying exactly what you mean, to have language without seams. At this moment you are doing the conversion, realizing the rate of exchange.

When your name is called you will first explain that you're sharing a single at the back of a hotel, near the *église* Saint-Sulpice, and the church bells often break conversation. You have a roommate named Pascale who wears braids like onyx pulled from her sharp face, her lips architecture in garnet. She's never surprised. A cigarette balanced with the index finger and thumb. If you told her, she'd want to know the name of the guy, *Comment il s'appelle d'ailleurs, ce mec qui t'a fait ça?* Pascale is no friend and besides, you can't tell her because you're not sure what his name was. Probably something hyphenated. Jean-Paul, Henri-Michel. What does it matter. Someone who taught you the subjunctive during those mornings that unravelled slowly, and he went *chez le boulanger* to get fresh bread, maybe a croissant, and he didn't return for hours, making you understand that you were supposed to leave.

Maybe it was that lawyer who never called back. He was the one who took you to Versailles on Armistice Day and knew a back way in, there was no one around, and you played hide and seek by that cottage with the water-mill, or maybe you just read about that? Sometimes it's hard to tell what you've actually done and what you spent a childhood dreaming of, but the part was real where the two of you got locked in after dark because he kissed you in a gazebo when you didn't know the right expression, or maybe you just used the wrong one on purpose, and he said, It's one of those charming things about American girls. As his lips pressed thickly onto yours you were thinking, strangely, of Marie Antoinette, how the sound of her skirts must have rushed in the wind as the autumn leaves did then.

Very soon after the lawyer there was another man, who wrapped his hands in your hair as if he were sinking and it was a lifeline and called its color *noir et feu,* black fire, and you thanked him. But he probably has nothing to do with this metal folding chair and this flat enamel wall and this silence, which is the heavy air created when women sit waiting to rid themselves of what they cannot bear. It is a secret too impossible to speak even to the woman in the next chair. She catches your eye and the look means I know, *je suis complice.*

—Mademoiselle Weeeelcoc? Sabine Wilcox? The nurse calls, eyes scanning the room for the figure belonging to that name.

—Present, you say. It is the same word in both languages, the French one just fluffier at the edges, a puff of a word.

Suddenly, as if overcome by nausea, you lean forward with a jerky motion to put your hands over your face, hoping that shutting out this room will transform it into a bad dream, thin enough to dissipate when you open your eyes. It doesn't work. There are always consequences: some things die, others live. I see you breathe out and sit up straight. What it comes down to is that for nineteen years you were just waiting for the break in the fence, for a chance to make your own life, and now how could you possibly be a mother, and everything that implies?

The question is, this multiplying cell (how much it feels like a cancer), or you, fully formed? You are going to say, *It's me who'll get out alive,* and you will not hesitate.

Chapter two

*V*otre carte d'assurance, s'il vous plaît, the nurse asks. Your insurance card.

—I don't have one (Do you say this in English? In French?).

She nods. What does it mean, that she just nods when you say you don't have one? Either she expected something like this from one such as you, or that it is acceptable not to have one.

She moves a piece of paper across the desk (the varnish thin and rough, too long without oil), pointing to the numbers at the bottom of the page with the metal tip of a ballpoint, as if by not saying the amount she disowns it, This charge is not my fault.

2100 F. That will mean about $400 American money, if the dollar holds next week.

You find yourself saying, That must be paid all at once? Next Monday? Her brows draw so close together it seems they will overlap. *Mais oui.* Of course.

—*Bien sûr.* Certainly, of course, yes. The money is paid up front by those not eligible for coverage under the government insurance. Certainly. Just checking. Of course.

Chapter three

Returning to the hotel on the snaky little alley called rue des Cannettes. Have to make sure the postcards are clearly visible, because if Madame Doumic, the concierge, asks, where have you been today, mademoiselle, are you not in school? you can tell her, I had the day off for good behaviour and walked the long walk across the bridge to Les Halles, shopped for postcards (can't ever get around to sending them).

You move quickly past the desk with eyes down but not quickly enough. The chair creaks and there is a popping, the sound of her knees grinding as her legs straighten.

—*Attendez, mademoiselle.* Madame Doumic's shoulders are rounded and she looks as if she's always about to bend down, but her hair is never less than carefully swept upwards, with black combs and a gold hairpin. The cloth of her cream blouse curves in folds and her skirt, always black or brown, drapes resolutely to her calf. Every day she is filled with imperatives, *il faut, vous devriez,* it is necessary, one must, you should. Often she assesses what you have, as in "You have mail" or "You have the rent?" But right now she only holds out her hand. Without ceremony she offers a small dried rose, its petals opened brazenly, exposing thin amber arms at the center.

—*Je vous offre cette eglantine.* It grew around the windows of my daughter's house. Vincennes, have you been there? Isn't it nice, this flower?

You repeat *eglantine?* because you don't know the word.

—*Très bien,* yes, she nods her head, offering encouragement. *C'est une rose sauvage,* it's a wild rose. She extends the flower.

—*C'est pour moi?* Is this for me? You are wary. You don't look her in the eye, convinced suddenly that somehow she knows, that it's written across your face, that anyone can tell.

—*Je vous en prie.* Please take it, she says, I have removed the thorns. In a starched English accented with the memory of summer trips across La Manche to London, Madame Doumic adds, Beauty is just for its own sake. It needs no special occasion.

Her parchment hands, the manicured oval of her ridged and yellowed nails. As she passes the stem, there is a fraction of time where fingers touch. The glow is warm. It lasts only a moment.

Chapter four

Idon't remember exactly what I had expected, but I do remember the sense when I arrived that everything here was reduced: the size of the cars, even the white stripe along the autoroute from de Gaulle into the city was narrower than any I had ever seen on a highway. How narrow too were the hands of the scholarship co-ordinator as they held the wheel. He was saying how fortunate it was for me he was bilingual. When he had studied in America decades ago, no one spoke anything but English. It had been hard for him, *dur,* as it is said. Yes, mademoiselle, you have much luck. He said, We will speak English in the car because it is evident you are tired.

—I really appreciate your thoughtfulness, I had said. But I was not at all tired, each nerve straining; I could smell the sound of the engine, I could hear the beige-brown-red of his overcoat lining.

The city did not thrust out of the horizon but rather gathered as an accumulation of buildings, squat and nameless at first but then growing more dense and grand. The streets were exactly as the pictures in my textbooks had detailed; I had sighed out loud and the man had not asked why. Or perhaps I did not make any noise, perhaps

I was silent and just tilted my face to the car window, pressing my forehead to the cool glass.

He deposited me in front of the hotel with a packet containing the address of the school and the syllabus, a city map, a chequebook for my scholarship money in a bank called Crédit Lyonnais, and the name of the concierge. This is what had been arranged for my year. Also there was the weight of a scratched brass key at the bottom.

—The key to the city? I smiled at him. I had tried to say it in French. Maybe I got it wrong. Maybe it wasn't funny.

—*Soyez prudente, mademoiselle,* Take care, the man replied. I advise you to make an effort to meet French people. If you meet only other Americans you will not learn to speak. I have seen it happen. It is a *piège,* a trap.

He did not offer to have lunch with me. There was no phone number in case there were problems. While he drove away I waited with my luggage on the sidewalk, I think one foot was in the street. I do not recall his name.

There is so much night and too little sleep. It leaves time to consider how Paris has been wrapped into a tight ball of one boulangerie, several streets and a handful of metro stops, at times one still bench in the park.

Right now it's near two in the morning and I have the volume turned down low on the black-and-white TV, the oyster light cast across the pilled bedspread. The TV is one of the luxuries, along with the bathroom and the sink, that make this studio plush beyond most student lodgings. It makes the room too expensive, beyond my allowance, which is almost gone. It is also why Pascale answered the small notice for "roommate wanted" on the bulletin board at school, the one I posted when it became clear the money would not stretch. The TV is why she gave me the deposit right away, even though she said I'd spelled things badly on the ad, and that told her I was of course an *étrangère,* no one but a foreigner could so mangle the verb agreement. She said, But at least you're not Arab. She said, These things must be considered.

I look over to her single bed pushed against the window, the exact fold of her sheets, the stark press of her black hair against such a white pillowcase. Pascale looks bored even in sleep. I wonder if she has ever been slapped. I pick one of the pills from the bed cover, pinch it tighter between my fingers and pitch it toward her bed, knowing it can't gain enough velocity to hit her, to actually make her brown eyes open, to make her say in that tinny way, *Qu'est-ce qu'il y a?* What is it?

This is the kind of sleep $400 buys.

*   *   *

On television a Frenchman wearing a leather motorcycle jacket and loafers is interviewing Iggy Pop about his life as a rock star. The man neglected to get a translator. What could he possibly need, after all, so sure that when "good", "is", "cool" and "punk" are strung together with enough French cognates they constitute English. Iggy has no idea what he is being asked, and he tells the man this and the man just laughs. So funny these Americans. And the man asks Iggy about his reputation for showing his penis on stage. Because the interviewer can only speak in the present tense Iggy thinks he is using the imperative, show your penis, show your penis. Iggy, craggy faced and amphetamine thin, looks disgusted and says, Alright man, if that's how you sick sons of bitches get off over here, what the hell. He stands up and pulls down his black jeans. Men like him never wear underwear.

Laughter comes over me, nearly startles me with the sound. I pull a pillow over my mouth and keep on. Pascale makes a small sound like a meow and turns over. I keep laughing into the pillow. Men like him. Damn.

The phone used to ring so early in the morning. Mom, tangled in the nylon nightgown she wore, never expecting to be alone, wouldn't be able to reach the receiver for so many rings and would yell, Bean? Bean, honey, grab that for me. By the time you got to her room she'd have picked up, but it would be the va hospital in El Paso calling about a problem with a Mr Nick Navarro. She'd say, I can't deal with this shit, and she would pass the phone to you, you would know what it was about, how Nick sometimes existed for days in a vapour and sometimes came back smelling like dirt and cheap weed and sometimes not. After you hung up she'd put her arms around you, tell you to lie with her, Your feet are like ice, come get warm. She would smooth the hair back from your forehead with her long fingers and say, Can't do much with men like him.

The program has ended, the screen shows nothing but a blizzard of static and that sound like fat spitting on coals. The city wrapped in night and no sign that morning is near.

Chapter five

You have been walking this goat path of a sidewalk every night from the boulevard Saint-Germain up to the Panthéon on insomniac rambles through the city, trying to extinguish the neon color that is sleeplessness, phosphorescent and annoying. Those hours when you catalogue the times you haven't measured up, when you feel the tension between your ribs and the weight of it in the moments before dawn.

Always when you pass the bar called The Crazy Violin, the same bartender is closing up. You observe him, the rhythmic sweep of his arms wiping away the yeasty-sticky residue of spilled drinks. You note the way he lingers, the cigarette he rubs between his forefinger and thumb. His lazuline eyes on you through the window. Even before tonight somehow you knew there had to be a sunburst pattern of lighter blue near the center.

The door is open. From behind the bar he walks over. He faces you, puts his hands on the edge of the pinewood sheen, his arms creating borders on either side of you, catching you in their frame.

—*Le cafard,* eh? Feeling down? he says. His words stay crisp at the corners, the tension in his jaw.

You relax your arms slightly, just enough to brush the sleeves of his shirt, just enough to feel the warmth emanating from his skin. That is all you really want.

—*Mal du pays,* you say, an easy way to make conversation. He will say, which country? And so it begins.

I consider what this can mean, to be homesick: sick of home, sick from home, sick about home. I have read about an illness called the Jerusalem Syndrome, where otherwise normal people visiting Israel suddenly believe they might be Christ or Mary. It is the not knowing for sure that tortures. The affliction is spontaneous, lasts only a few days. When they leave, the disease disappears. It could be the sun, an allergy to mica in that sand, perhaps the scent of dung burning in open fires that creates the maladjustment, the particular sense of dislocation in Jerusalem. I have never been there, so I can only guess. But I keep coming back to this idea, that geography inspires psychosis.

So somehow you start talking about where you're from. Partly it is for the beauty of the words off your tongue, your power to form them, ground to a clear polish, finely executed. The occasional hairline fractures make it exciting for the listener.

But more than that, tonight you are remembering the scorched summer air of home and the way you wished for reptile lungs. By talking about it maybe you will understand why an accidental truck-stop off an interstate can resonate inside a heart, the way the Organ Mountains rise, a pair of wolf's teeth against the even topography of the mesas. Land expands as far as regrets, cut by the malachite ribbon of the Rio Grande valley. How, when you look into the desert with your pale eyes you see the blush of trailing windmills, yellow spiny daisies, explosions of globemallow and the burnt blossoms of threadleaf groundsel.

The slipface of a sand dune is supposed to be the most lifeless environment on earth, but you have seen different. Even there bleached, earless lizards make forked patterns on the sand crust and Apache pocket mice build homes. You have witnessed the sometime triumph of the sumac's deep roots holding back the shifting dunes that swell from the gypsum flaking off alkali flats, carried by wind.

The bartender listens for a long time and you realize his eyes are a blue that don't make you think of the sky.

—France is nothing like that, he says finally.

—I can tell.

He says the bar is closed but you can stay for a drink (and here his voice hovers, uncertain) if you'll come down to the cellar with him.

You hesitate, so as not to seem eager.

—Yes. I would like a drink.

He reaches for your hand going down the slick grade of stairs to the cellar, says *attention*, be careful. When he feels your hand, feather-down to the touch, willing to give, he becomes suddenly bold, eager as men will be. At the base of the stairs he pulls you against him (at least he is tall, you like that) and presses his fist into the small of your back, tilting your head, throat exposed as if to say, kill me now. He smoothes his lips along your jaw.

His other hand seems to melt over your collar bone, warm as wax running between your breasts and then down toward your stomach.

—*Non!* You jerk away. Don't touch me there.

He stands frozen, at once uncertain and exposed. If you could see his eyes through this darkness he would look confused as a boy. *Où ça,* he asks, where?

You recover, take his straining fullness in your hand.

—*Comme ça,* you say, in one supple move lifting your skirt and rubbing him against you. Touch me like this.

And now this black clay rubbed into your knees, crusting your palms, the smell of dead earth. The thin shiver where his sweat wets your back and how the cellar draft sucks it off your skin. Your breasts swing heavily, aching. He cups one and squeezes; it hurts. You reach back, scratching and pulling his haunches deeper in. His body is taut, well defined; his skin has the scent of a pack animal, and when he pulls your hair back (all that hair) he nips your ear and bites your lips, and his tongue is strong, filling your mouth.

He releases. Your hair hangs in a curtain over your face. Maybe today you will sleep.

Chapter six

Stepping out the door and turning up the street. Lips bruised from pressing, beard stubble raising a kind of rash along my neck. Feeling briny and chapped from the friction. I know how this ripped skirt must look. This is not something that would hold up in sunlight. Thankfully there is no one else on the street at 4 AM This is the best time, the hem of night that no one notices.

Can it be that you have been up for days, or is this just one long day that will eventually end, or is this perhaps the kind of dream you can't wake up from? That's what it feels like. And each street is the same, gray bricks, gray walls, gray sky. Years from this moment, when you think back on this place, maybe all you will remember is the absence of color.

I trace bricks with my finger as I walk. The truth of the matter is that I have never had many talents, but of those I do possess the strongest has always been the ability to catalogue precisely what composes my life. The parameters used to include one long irrigation ditch, a family cobbled from one mother, one boyfriend bartender as make-shift father, satellites of their estranged relatives, a series of ponies, used books, school, Miss Ortiz and her niece, Mia, my best friend. But those no longer hold, and with each of these gray mornings I feel my ability leeching away. Now I am not much different from a bug, assessing the world through feelers, measuring texture, attuned to the tension of molecules hanging suspended. I don't hear so much as register frequency.

It is still so early when I return to the hotel that Madame Doumic is not at the desk and I have to use the code to buzz myself through the door, a carved, chipped green that once must have looked good to the Germans.

Light seeps through the shutters when I enter the room. The door hinges whine.

—Sabine? Pascale's voice calls, tinted by irritation.

—*Oui. C'est moi,* I tell her, my back turned, unbuttoning my shirt.

—*Tu as bien fait la fête?* Did you have fun partying?

I shrug. Uh huh.

—*Tu n'a jamais peur?* You don't ever get afraid? she asks, but I understand this is a Sophist's technique, these questions are aimed at another point entirely. As a rule we do not talk to each other; she keeps her life tightly contained, never spilling over into mine, as if afraid of contamination. I assume she's noticed my skirt.

—*Je fais comme je veux,* I do what I want. I slip into bed, too achy and bloodshot even to bathe.

She talks on, says she noticed I didn't go to class yesterday. She says, Have you had the stomach flu? She couldn't help but notice. Is it catching? I answer, no, it's not catching. Just something I ate. *Je dors,* I tell her, I'm going to sleep now.

My eyes are wide open. I suck my finger, raw at the tip from running over bricks.

Tuesday

Chapter seven

Imagine this: it comes with no warning, a shrill bleating, right in your ear, without words and slightly hysterical. Then it comes again, more like a buzzer this time, and you're instantly awake, as if someone's telling you the bed is on fire. This is instinct, how to pick up quickly, to not care about knocking the phone off the night-stand, the clang and ding as it hits the carpet, the winding cord made straight by the shock of the sudden weight.

You just grab the receiver as if it were a throat and say, Hello? but it is not so much a question as an accusation. Hello? you say again, slower this time, trying to sort from among the thousands possible the next words you could say. You can't tell which is English and which is French. In the morning it's always so hard to remember where you are.

—*Allô, j'écoute.*

No response from the other end, just a hiss and crackle coming off the line, faint echoes of other conversations bleeding over. An overseas call.

—Hi? Mom? Is this you? Your head pounds from rising too fast. You hear your own breath fill the receiver.

Above the static on the line there seems to be a meek greeting, but maybe you're just anticipating the hairpin curve of her voice, those gravelly banks.

The line crackles again but more surely this time you hear, Bean? Can I speak-ez to Bean? She puts on her idea of a French accent, thinking it makes her English immediately understandable.

—It's me, Mom. Now you retrieve the phone from the floor.

—Hey, baby! she says, and you can hear immediately that she's trying to act straight. Bean, I can't tell the difference between you and your little roommate anymore, with you talking like that.

There is no possible response and in these cases you know to let the silence build. Nature abhors a vacuum; soon it will become uncomfortable and she will rush to fill the space.

—Well, I just called to see how you are, baby. I miss you, she says, and you know that she does. If her voice were an instrument it would be an alto sax, the kind of sound that even when played brightly hints at the weepy note to come.

—I'm Alright. Good. I mean, things are a little tight, you begin, but it doesn't matter how much you want to tell her. If you said, can you send some money? (even $50 would help, you can eat on that for a while), she would say, Sure, what for? And you would say, A procedure, and then she would want to know the kind of procedure, she would want to know the exact terminology the doctor had used. You couldn't make something up because she'd press for more details, she's a nurse, she knows the right questions to ask. And then you could not stand the long sigh, the heavy, knowing pause, the resignation that this sort of catastrophe was inevitable. Then she would say something like, God, I've really let you down, and you would rush to reassure her that she's done nothing, she is faultless, that you will make everything Alright.

It was the night that marked one year since everything happened with Nick. I was leaving the following Wednesday. I had eaten dinner at Mia's house and when I came home she was curled up in the bathroom, the cigarette butt melting more holes in her nightgown. I bent down to pick her up, tendrils of her platinum hair lying thinly across her moist cheek. She stared blankly, her green eyes ill-focused and filmy, as if she were looking up from underwater. She raised a hand to brush it limply across my face before it fell away from the exhaustion of the effort. The strength of her voice was startling when she spoke.

—I always want to tell you so much. But I just, I have nothing to say.

I cradled her head in my lap. She said, You're not going to leave me, right, baby? Tigers breed true. You're my tiger.

I think I leaned my back against the toilet, I remember the weight of her head pressing into my leg.

—Say it! she yelled suddenly, hitting my thigh with her wet palm. Say you're my tiger!

—I'm your tiger, I said, and instantly she relaxed, her lips curling in an approximation of a smile. Her eyes closed. The weight of her head became heavier.

On the phone now she's somehow got onto the subject of Nick. You knew it would come sooner or later.

—I miss the bastard so much, Beanie, so much, God, why? She doesn't even try to sound sober any more, breathing like a woman keening through a bad air. The line cracks and snaps with static.

—Hello? Sorry, I can't hear. Call next week. I'm hanging up now, you shout, too loudly. There is a series of sharp clicks, she's saying, Okay, I love you baby. Then, silence.

You lie back, still holding the phone as it starts to beep-beep-beep, off the hook.

Chapter eight

I'm walking by the river this morning, again, and it's raining, again, and drops fall through my collar and down the thicker, oilier skin of my back. Feel them sliding, evaporating. People pass with umbrellas, with raincoats made from that indefinite shade of taupe, scarves colored tan and brown, women in wide plaid. They don't even try to pretend they're not staring, me just in jeans and a cotton blouse. Shivering in the rain is a feeling I have grown to like, so often do I misjudge the clouds here and get caught without protection. I have never been this wet in my life; in the high desert I never knew rain without thunder and lightning.

Today there was a postcard from home in the mail slot by Madame Doumic's desk. I round it in my palm as the paper reverts to pulp, the crooked pen lines turning to thin, blue rills, running down my arm. Mia sent this card picturing the old bandstand in the plaza. A sunny day, the chrome glare off the old cars frozen by the camera. I had looked for my mother's car in the photo, a rag-topped white Mustang, cracked Naugahyde. She calls the car "Mariah", refers to it as "old girl", still doesn't like it when I drive her. There is no clear indication what year it was taken, everything always seems out of date, not like Las Cruces, the surrounding town that runs like a sleeve up the interstate, kept current by its mini malls, chain restaurants and stores. Finding Mesilla requires a couple more turns off the main roads, it's the kind of place people don't come to unless they have a reason, or unless they've somehow been turned around.

Before the rain the card had read:

> Dear Beanie, You may be in gay Paree but me, Angel and Rina got tickets to the Whitesnake concert in El Paso! You jealous or what? Check this out: Rose Torres, the Rose who lives near your mom, brought home curtains from the Walmart. They weren't out of the bag more than an hour before she's saying she sees the Virgin Mary on them. She wants to charge admission because everyone's lining up but Father Harvey says she's got to call it a donation to the Church or its a sin. Miss you! Write more! Mia.

In Mesilla encounters with God are fortuitous but difficult to categorize. One year the face of Jesus reveals itself on a tortilla, now the Virgin on polyester, her image effulgent, illuminating Rosa's living room in a glowing chartreuse. Mom will drop in to consider the evidence. In her own bedroom there will still be the jade bead rosary and its protective sheath of dust. On her dresser the collection of candles Nick gave her, ones for St Martin, the Virgin and St Jude, patron saint of the hopeless and the one she used to light the most. There are a few chubby buddhas, a Koran scroll, one Balinese goddess figure. It is important to have options. Things don't always work out. She says, Cover all the bases.

Father Harvey organizes the demonstrations in front of the clinic where my mom works. He never seems angry so much as terribly disappointed, as if it would be easy to make him cry. He's the only person who calls me Sabine.

Priests like Father Harvey don't seem to exist in France. Here, where everyone is Catholic, when a woman does not want to have a child it is considered a routine medical procedure, much like the extraction of a wisdom tooth. Or perhaps a cancer. Yes. The unchecked division of cells, the uncontainable multiplication.

At the Café Odéon there are empty tables by the window, so I duck in, sit down, dripping wet on the rattan weave of the little chair. A paper napkin has been left on the table. When the waiter passes I look vaguely in his direction and say *Un espress.* This will cost as much as I should spend at the UniPrix for groceries. I live on boiled pasta and gruyère, but the smell of wheat in hot water has started to make me sick.

When the waiter returns with the coffee (over which no steam rises), I ask to borrow his pen and he actually pulls one from his apron, extending it towards me. The act so effortless, as if generosity were a reflex for him, stills my reach for a second. It is a second too long. He shrugs and retracts the pen, never breaking stride.

—*Merci quand même,* thanks anyway, I say under my breath.

In front of me suddenly is another pen. The hand extending it belongs to an older man, short-legged and broad-shouldered, his pinkie nearly as long as his index finger, making his hand square. His face is grainy, a collection of odd parts. His cheekbones form a high ridge that creates an open plane.

—*C'est gentil,* That's very kind of you. I only need it for a minute, I tell him, this time quickly snatching the pen, in case he too should change his mind. He nods and sits down at the next table. Our chairs butt, his elbow nudges mine. I pretend not to notice and begin writing on the napkin in small letters, lightly, careful not to tear.

Dear Mia: When it rains Paris smells like dog shit, and right now it's raining. The sidewalks are landmines of crap. They take their dogs into grocery stores; they eat raw apples with a knife and fork. Paradox is sophistication (yes I made that up, no I didn't read that in a book). I have stopped trying to master apple cutting because I keep shooting it off the plate.

This fills the napkin square. When I look up again the man's gaze aims at the street.

Merci de votre generosité. I appreciate your kindness, I say as I slip the pen onto his table.

Pas de quoi, You're welcome, he replies, but turns his eyes on me with a needling look, better called dissection, I feel some process of evaluation occurring. I glance down to see if my buttons are ordered in a straight line. I wonder if the espresso's cold foam clings to the edge of my lips.

Monsieur, I begin, not sure where I am going with this. *Monsieur,* I was writing a letter and I was just wondering about different things, and have you ever seen the Virgin Mary? I mean, on a living-room curtain?

His eyebrow raises in mild surprise, the corner of his mouth tilts upward. He presses his lips together before he speaks. *Jamais,* mademoiselle. Indeed, never.

* * *

This man with the badlands face says he is amazed at my accent, but what he means is my lack of accent, this kinesthetic ability to hold my jaw with the correct stress, pressing my tongue to my teeth at the precise intervals. He is certain I am not French but I can tell he doesn't know exactly what I am, and this perturbs him. How, exactly, did I learn French?

—Princeton, I tell him, inclining my head with a slight tilt, my tone knowing. I learned it at Princeton.

I might as well say Mars for as close to the truth as that is, but it is an easier image to hold. This stranger. The raindrops still dripping off my cuff. He seems to consider my explanation, as if turning it in his mind. I understand that he is looking for a blood connection to the culture, so I add, And my father is Belgian, that is, *wallon.*

It is unbelievable to the French that an American could truly crack the codes and be allowed entrance to their language. They say this does not happen often and I believe them. I have heard language stripped, like gears grinding, reduced painfully. I have come to believe communication is a question of sacrifice; the effort it takes to inhabit a new language demands a willingness to recast yourself and forfeit the bedtime stories that fed you, abandon other delicate things that made you. Speaking a new language fluently is to tamper with foundations. It cannot be undertaken lightly.

The Frenchman shrugs, seems unconvinced. *Alors, où est l'accent belge,* Where's the accent?

—Did I say Belgian? I didn't mean that literally, I say, pretending to be flustered. My mother just always called him a dumb Belgian. I lean forward and whisper, You know how it is with parents.

He is openly suspicious but intrigued, turning his chair towards mine. The current of his breath is near; his mouth smells like butter, smooth but always the possibility of turning rancid. He wants to know if I was raised bilingual. He says there is a hint of something he cannot place.

I consider how to answer. My first French lessons came from my mother's bathroom shelf, reading the labels of her perfumes in their colored glass swirls. She would not let me touch because the shelf was full of voodoo, civilization was conjured there. Without it men would be lost in the wilderness, turn feral and eat their own in any meagre season.

But that is not what he's asking. The rhythm this man hears is Spanish, how those words shaped me when my bones were still the soft bones of a child, rubbing against English, intertwining on my tongue. There was Nick and the sharp geometry of his uniform, the scent of metal stitching, back from his second tour of Vietnam. He bought me an organdy dress but it was toddler size. His voice a thin string, asking, How old are you now, *mi hijita?*

The man is staring at me, waiting for a response, but I just look away. It's a move Madame Doumic makes. Keep your mouth shut and people will think you have more to say.

—*Etudiante?* he says. A clear change of subject, meaning, so you are a student? Just a label, life so readily falling into class, kind, division.

I nod and ask him what he does. To his ears this sounds impudent, crass, someone my age asking him to state himself for the record.

With a meandering gesture he hands me his personal card. Jean Praquin, phone number.

—*On peut dire que je cherche la forme de la vie.* One could say I look for the shape of life.

—*Drôle de metier,* I reply, What a weird line of work. I avoid touching his fingers as I pocket the card and ask, You actually get paid to do that?

He shrugs. *De temps en temps.* From time to time.

We sit beside each other with nothing to say. Finally he clears his throat.

—*Ecoutez, mademoiselle,* Listen, he says. Granite is the color of his eyes. You look *fauché comme les blès* and I have work.

Fauché comme les blès, cut like the wheat, literally. That is to say, broke, broke, broke. I fold my arms across my chest, at this minute acutely aware of how it must look to walk in the rain dressed as I am.

—Monsieur Praquin, are you offering me work?

—That depends. We will have to see.

Chapter nine

You have a class this afternoon but you are going to miss it. You will not bother to change your clothes, still sodden and cold. You're going to meet Jean Praquin at this address because you said you would, though you don't know why. He scares you. He is balding, he smells of boiled cabbage. You've noticed there are no plumb lines to his fingers, as if each has been broken and badly recast. The top of his head hits your armpit. His shoe-box build. His offer to you at the Café Odéon. He probably lies.

So, you take your time. Walk across the Jardin du Luxembourg, avoiding the pinkstone paths, cutting right through the grass, hoping a *gardien* will try to stop you because you want to yell at someone, anyone. But no one notices, as if your skin is transparent when backlit by noon.

You stop at a wheeled vending cart selling crêpes because that will take time, too, make you even more late. Maybe he'll give up and leave.

—Just butter and sugar please, you tell the *vendeuse* who was selling chestnuts last week. Or maybe you're just thinking that because

her hair falls in one straight bolt of chestnut that looks as if it's waiting to be woven. She smiles when she presents the crêpe, its tissue
already yellowed and slick with butter, but you've been practising
this. You don't smile back as you take your change.

The crêpe's sugar-grains roll against the enamel of your teeth,
making them ache, and you take that as evidence of decay. Bad teeth.
Even, straight, but prone to rot, and the discoloration speckled over
the front two caused by an overabundance of fluoride in the water
you drank as a child. The ache could indicate a more recent development, how your body is already being robbed of calcium. The leeching
away at your core.

You've been eating and walking too fast and suddenly, here you
are, standing at the wooden gate where his address is numbered. This
place once a stable or a carriage house, you can't tell, and you're not
prepared to see him. You reach to touch the wide grain of the wood;
God but it must be two hundred years old and nobody has kicked it
in. You want to press your nose against it to see if the scent of bark
lingers or if its been choked by the oil of too many fingers.

There are always stairs in France, and you climb those before
you now. You stand at his door, which has no carving or other elabo-
ration, just a glassy hole in the center. Closing your eyes, inhaling.
From under the door there seeps the sunburst aroma of neroli. It must
be incense he burns. Evidently he has made coffee, too, because you
detect the warm, muscular smell of a fresh pot. This is an unantici-
pated measure of hospitality.

Praquin opens the door without your knocking and says Hello,
the word sounding unwieldy and bulky because he can't pronounce
the English "h". You step into a large room with a generous window
and notice how its thick, aged glass warps light. Canvases in varying
shapes and states of attention lean near brushes and jars and tools
that look like finer versions of those that hang from a carpenter's
belt, and a large clump of earthen material is piled on a rough table.
Near the window a small spigot drips hard water into the porcelain,
worn dull and porous as old bones. You move to sit on the only soft
surface, a futon covered in tired China silk.

—*Non,* he tells you. Stand. *Comme ça. Oui.* And you're not sure what he wants. You think this is the reason he scares you, you can't easily divine his intentions.

He asks you to take off your shirt.

—*Comment?* What? You ask him, not believing you understood correctly.

He points to his own shirt and says, This. Take yours off. All this as if it were casual conversation, as if he were saying, please, make yourself at home.

When you don't move he sort of smiles and says, You don't understand. I'm an artist. Now take off your shirt. If I wanted to fuck you, don't you think I'd try harder?

—Tell me you're queer.

He ignores this, talking as if you have not spoken. He tells you, By the way, don't ever wear white again, *ça te va pas,* there is no harmony with your skin.

There may be some sense in that, so you take off your shirt, and he motions like, Take off the bra, and now you don't want him to think you're cowed by him so you do that, too.

—*Quoi encore,* you say, trying for a brash tone that rings much too hollow. What now?

—*Tais toi,* he says, Be quiet (much too familiar). He reaches out to move his thick-skinned thumb along the fishbelly smoothness of your arms, slowly measuring the sharpness of your collarbone, the curve of your chin, and then he considers the uneven slope of your breasts.

And the pants, he says, seeming preoccupied, but this might be some sick trick so you tell him No way, even though you know you're going to do it anyway, because you need the money and because there is something that wants to know how deep the descent will be for you, how steep the grade. As you stand there feeling round and overfat he circles you silently, runs the thumb along your back and into the dimpled wells of your tailbone, and seems to be contemplating something else entirely. Perhaps you have misjudged; perhaps you stand before the kind of man who has no expectation. You are waiting for the moment when his touch will become recognizable, transmits a need you can comprehend but that touch doesn't come, so you stand there, wondering what to do with your hands.

He goes over to his table, grabs a black charcoal and smoothes something across a page.

—*Bravo, ma douce.* He says, his voice deep. He turns from you and adds in a way that invites no response, Your lines are what I'm looking for. You will work for me. Start tomorrow.

Chapter ten

Although the morning rain clouds have made way for a brighter afternoon, I am not fooled. This anaemic sun will soon fall to night.

I take the route along the Seine back from Praquin's, thinking maybe I'll go all the way to the Marais just for something to do. But it's too cold, my clothes will not dry, and suddenly all I want is sleep. I should have taken the metro, at the very least walked along Saint-Germain. Now I have to go all the way the river (a canal, more rightly said) to rue Bonaparte and walk until it runs into the place Saint-Sulpice. The wind hits my neck and spreads a chill, raising skin like beads down my spine.

Maybe I've missed the street already, walking with my head down. I stop and look for someone who might offer direction but there is just a very old man, stoop-shouldered and smoking a Gauloise, skin paunchy and grayed by fumes. He walks a small boxy dog with a curly-q tail and pug face.

—*Pardonnez-moi, monsieur.* I bend forward slightly, trying to catch his eye.

He doesn't alter his shuffling pace, but the dog stops to face me squarely, its black ears alert. The man just jerks its thick neck with a leather leash smooth from wear. *Viens, ma puce,* Come along pretty girl, he murmurs thickly to the dog.

Two women walking arm in arm pass me. One looks as old as the man but walks ramrod straight, as if her body were saying to anyone who noticed, look, pride knows no years. The other is younger but her face is lined, her wool cape a cerise billow in the wind. Their heads are turned in opposite directions. I never seem to catch French women in the act of talking to each other. I slow my pace to look at the two, wondering if either one has ever braided the other's hair.

I remember my mother putting the fragrances behind her ears, on her wrists, on the slick, white skin on the backs of her knees. Slowly, as if anointing. Closing her eyes, inhaling deeply. I would string the names together for her as if I were reading poetry, *Muguets des Bois, Je Reviens, Arpège, L'Air du Temps, eau de toilette.* She would laugh, her skin flushing. She'd start to tickle me and sing, Oh they don't wear pants in the southern part of France.

She always pulled me closer as she sat at the bench of her dressing table so we were eye-to-eye, taking a perfume bottle from my hand to set it gently on the wood. She would put her hands on my shoulders and say, *You are going to do things I never did, baby, and when you do, you just remember that you're my eyes. You'll be seeing all those great things for me.*

In those days, I wondered what she meant.

By the time I get back to the rue des Cannettes the first hint of dusk has settled. Pascale sits hunched on her bed writing something for a class, her nose close to her notebook. She doesn't look up.

For my dinner there's a head of lettuce, a day-old baguette and moldy cheese that I may or may not have bought that way. I take the one large bowl from the top of the waist-high refrigerator and start to make a vinaigrette.

—*Ça ne se fait pas comme ça,* it's not done like that, Pascale calls from the bed, her tone exasperated, as if my very breathing offends some etiquette I never knew existed.

—*Comment ça?* Like what? I ask, extending the wooden spoon toward her. *Dis-moi,* Tell me.

The two of us stand looking at the bowl, as if it will provide the next words. She seems to be waiting for something, but what? For lack of anything else I toss the leaves, stalling as I try out different sentences in my head. In the months we've lived together in this one room, we have never shared such a moment. Nothing is allowed to bleed over. She hides her muesli under her bed. Thinks I don't notice. Sometimes, I eat it anyway.

Her child-size hand quickly brushes me out of the way. She ignores the spoon and instead reaches for one of our three forks while she dumps the white-green butter-lettuce leaves from the bowl onto the dishtowel, bleached thin. *Regarde,* she says, a simple command. Watch. She glances up to make sure my attention is focused. Her eyes are soft and her mouth turned pleasantly, not the commitment of a smile perhaps but the same intent.

She takes a teaspoon of that grainy mustard the color of dried leaves, plops it with the fork into the bowl and follows it with shakes of salt and pepper. Tu vois? See what I'm doing now? She says as she whisks a dollop of grapeseed oil into the mustard. *Pas difficile.* I nod gravely, say, Yes, it's not hard. Yes, I think I'm getting it now.

She wastes no single movement, so mechanical in her precision. It occurs to me that this is the kind of certainty bred into people after hundreds of years. I imagine Pascale standing at her mother's apron, learning this same lesson as it has always been repeated. Maybe there are no words exchanged, perhaps it is just a series of observations, with Pascale's black eyes wide and expecting the comfort of predictable action. All at once a kind of tenderness engulfs me, threatens to buckle my knees. She can be nothing more than she is in this moment. There is an awkward impulse to hug her around the shoulders, but how would that be explained? I just stand beside her, breathing the layers of her perfume, so very much taller than she, coltish and mute.

—Not a lot of vinegar. Always remember three of oil to one of vinegar, she cautions, letting it gently dribble into the bowl, the slight acidic smell, like something left out too long. I crinkle my nose.

—*Et puis un peau d'eau pour que le vinaigre ne soit pas trop fort,* Then a little bit of water so the vinegar won't be too strong, her voice still that kindergarten-teacher nice. She holds the spoon over the tap as the water fills its shallow groove, then splashes it over the mixture. Whisk, whisk. Metal fork scrapes glass. She puts the lettuce leaves back in the bowl, tossing them with the fork until each is glossed with a coat of vinaigrette. *Voilà.*

—*L'eau, c'est le secret de chef, Pascale?* Water is your secret? The sound of my own voice makes me jump; I had not realized I wanted to say anything until I heard myself already talking.

She looks up at me, nods, the crescent of her smile now definite. *Mon secret.*

Finally I say, It's not much, but do you want to eat something with me?

She says *C'est sympa, d'accord,* Okay, nice of you to ask. I move to sit at the small table while she gets a plate and another glass. I shut the wooden shutters and realize, I am no longer tired. This moment, so unexpected, so perfectly formed.

Wednesday

Chapter eleven

T

*he dream begins with a silver ladle spilling onto a hardwood floor,
you running your thumb across Irish crystal, the whining pitch of glass,
and then you're making her cry. You see her skin, cream rich, thick like
lace and linen too long folded in a drawer, smelling finely dusted with
powder and crusty sugar. And then you realize, she is everything old. There
is a scent of burning pinon and all at once you're in the barn, the stack
of firewood, the rusting hoe. Then there is only red, a twitching, the click
and slide, and suddenly your heart is beating.*

I wake up like that, just like running in the dark, shaken and wet. My
face is pressed against the stone wall that borders the bed, my cheek
numb, as if laid on ice, the outline of rock indenting my face. I reach
up to trace the jutting edges, the gray mortar crumbles silently and
falls in a fine grit to the bed cover.

    —*Qu'est-ce qu'il y a?* What's the matter? Pascale's voice. Its small
tone with no resonance. Makes me think of a porcelain bell Mom
gave me once with "Greetings from Pecos, Texas" in rolling painted
script on one side, a picture of a bronc rider on the other.

—*Rien,* Nothing, I tell her, pulling the blankets tighter around.

Pascale is ready for school, her hair held back with a cloth band and secured with clips. The order appears random but that is the secret of being French, the covert deliberateness. I think of the sweatshirts and jeans I wore to class those first weeks, how Pascale must have thought they were contagious. As if by proximity she'd develop a craving for ketchup, neglect to wear the right shoes. This makes me laugh. Her brows knit together and she turns away, miffed, as if somehow she missed a joke.

—*Je rêvais,* I was dreaming, I say, softly, an effort to reach across whatever always separates us. But she is already too far away, and now she is out the door, shutting it quietly. I hear the tap, tap of her patent leather heels fall across the sagging oak of the stairs. For an instant I have the urge to follow her, tell her about my dream, but I let it pass because if I were to build another bridge to her, then what? Would we be best friends, share clothes, trade lipstick? Would she cry to me when her boyfriend from Marseilles doesn't call? Would I tell her?

No.

I lie hugging the firm pillow. Praquin expects me at nine. A seminar I haven't attended in two weeks begins at the same time. I don't move to do either but instead reach under my bed to my suitcase. A letter from my grandmother is pressed against the bottom, under my nice summer dress and a coat Mom bought me. The French call it *moche,* too ugly to wear.

I grope for the tissue feel of the pages, I can see the fine slant of her letters written in narrow black lines. It is the only thing she has written me.

Dear Bean,

It is the end of summer. Soon I have to plant bulbs. I have noticed that the roof is in bad shape, and it looks like time for a few new spruce beams. I am thinking about you in Paris. Napoleon said, "Come to Paris and become a woman."

I read that in *Vogue* once. It was an article about how to wear red. I have always remembered that.

I'm glad you're out of that place, but honestly I still don't know what you're going to do with all that French. I don't know why everybody wants to go to Europe when our ancestors couldn't wait to get out of it.

I say, "big deal." I've been on the train up to Montreal a few times and it doesn't do a damn thing for me.

Anyhooo… They say the sun causes cataracts, and I think they are right because I can't read as good as I once did. It is from that time in the desert. I can't tell you how glad I am to be back in Boston.

Take care of yourself. Your mother had a lot of potential too until she went off out West. I hope you're still the good girl you were brought up to be. You have a wonderful opportunity to make a life for yourself.

Love,
Your Grand

I bring the feather-skin page to my nose, inhale. She believes a woman of substance should spray her fragrance on stationery as a form of silent punctuation, and indeed this one floats in *L'Air del Tropic,* an old favorite heavy with the suggestion of magnolia and other blossoms that are native to nowhere I've ever been.

August is the end of a wicked season in that stretch of country where New Mexico meets West Texas. The sky is too bold, wind always blows at the airport, the kind that whips fine grains against the skin, scours the eyes. Trees grow no leaves and the lilacs twining the porch fade, their perfume evaporating in the heat.

The day the plane arrived from Boston, my mother and I stood braced with backs against a wall outside the terminal, my mother with a leg bent and the heel of her boot against the plaster, hair piled loosely on her head, platinum strands drooping like dried stalks down her neck. Arms folded across her chest. A stream of passengers walked by, marked as new arrivals by their paleness, the squint of their eyes shielding against the first burning, true sun. Mom called out to a passing woman, silhouetted by a black, angular skirt and a shirt the white of gypsum or salt.

—So. You survived the trip. Mom exhaled her cigarette through her nose as she said this, a cloud forming around her face. She reached to hold my hand though I had long since become too big for that. She pulled me forward and I felt the ruby lacquer of her nails slick against my palm.

The woman turned and surprised with her smile, wide like something people need a bridge to get over, her lips drawn precisely end to end. Her hair was the first time I saw the color mahogany; she wore it straight, cropped at the shoulders with bangs and later in the car she would explain her more than passing resemblance to a woman named Gene Tierney, a movie star I had never heard of. This would surprise her, and she would ask my mother, Don't you teach this child anything? I would learn she was the kind of woman who put on clothes as if dressing were an act requiring a formula, and she had special names for every garment, every hook and eye and liner, even the straps on shoes.

But at this moment, as she walked toward me, all that I knew was she moved unlike anyone I had ever seen, as if caught by a breeze, gracile, landing lightly, skin like white rose petals, milky.

—Nothing green here, is there? By God, it looked like a Moon landing, she said. Her words tumbled forward with a rhythm not familiar, her English different from the sound I knew it to have. The woman was saying, I felt like Neil Armstrong. You know, I smell the blue in the sky here, there's so much of it. Give me a hug, by God.

The woman held out her arms and Mom bent forward, but their intersection was painful, a collision. The woman moved to press her red mouth against her cheek, but Mom pulled away and said, Let's not push it.

The woman didn't respond, just kept smiling. She turned to

face me, reaching out to rub the back of her hand across my jaw. I wondered if I would get into trouble for pressing against the smooth texture of her skirt, as if she were something breakable. Against the seared horizon this woman appeared as a hothouse flower, about to disintegrate in the direct sunlight, would bruise brown if held with a strong grip.

—And I bet I know who this is! The woman said, her lips never seeming to move across the vast whiteness of her teeth.

Mom put her hand on my shoulder, propelling me forward.

—Sabine, she said, this is Siobàn Wilcox. Your grandmother. She's related to you.

I was unprepared for the concept. There was Nick, his sister Dahlia who I called Tia, there were our neighbors, old men at the bar. There was Mia even then, but my mother existed outside of it all, unconnected, a silver light creating her own orbit.

—What part of me is she related to? I asked, because I really was curious. Mom remained silent while the woman laughed, the sound from her throat like copper windchimes.

—Call me Grandma, sweetie. Or Grand. Such a pretty face you have. What coloring! You have big gray eyes like some old owl.

She looked at Mom and raised her eyebrow, saying, I tell you, she doesn't look Spic. I mean, thank God. No one would even guess.

Mom seemed to lose her bearing, stunned, gaping as if recovering from a blow to the side of the head.

—At least you're consistent, the words from my mother's mouth arrived pressed from between clenched teeth.

—I meant...

—This is a mistake.

—I only want to help.

—Don't do me any favors. Mom yanked my hand, pulling me so tight against her leg. Just go back. I'll go back to considering you dead.

I started to cry, a feeling of rupture and a stone-like sinking, wondering if all this was my fault.

—Enough, my grandmother said, and she wasn't smiling anymore. I'm no good at transitions. Let's try this again, shall we?

And then she had me in her arms, but my mother never let go of my hand. The three of us walked forward, without speaking.

Chapter twelve

Y ou really mean to go to class today. Forget about Praquin. There's got to be another way. You'll sit in that beige-walled chamber with DEFENSE DE FUMER painted in red but everybody lighting up anyway, the cigarette air stinking under fluorescent lights. You'll sit next to that brunette girl with perspiration and dirt collecting in the thin rings around her neck, the one who color-codes her notes in blue and purple. You are going to draw pictures of flowers with weirdly proportioned petals off the green margins of your notebook, take notes half in English, half in French, all spelt badly. You will listen to the lecturer, mimic his tones and inflection until someone throws you a sidelong look, realize you're mumbling. Then you'll stop and try to pay attention to whatever the lecturer is saying.

But when you actually get to the flat steps of the building, modular and ugly (you think it might be called modernist archi- tecture, but you'd have to look it up to say for sure), you have that same, overwhelming, deflated sense. There were supposed to be wide arches, refined, old window-panes with a view of all the shades of gray Paris is. You had imagined holding the worn leather binding of books with pages like yellowing pearls and having someone tell you more about Baudelaire and Rimbaud, talk about whatever people talk about in universities. But this is not the Sorbonne and the halls have linoleum tiles.

On the steps a fellow student in a skirt and turtleneck sweater brushes past, her arms long and thin as PVC pipes, her skin clear, her nose large. You offer a small *bonjour.* She regards you (not even a flicker of response), then turns away.

You know this is a moment that must be recorded: the exact instant you decide to never, ever go back to class. What didn't you think of this before? They can't take your scholarship away, you're already here, the money mostly spent. If explanations are demanded you'll just say you had a breakdown, you'll say the membrane between dreaming and waking ruptured.

You arrive at Praquin's studio not more than ten minutes late, breathless from running, not ringing the bell, taking the stairs two at a time, landing heavily on the steps (an observer might say, "as if to dislodge something"). You wonder what Praquin's reaction will be, whether he worried over whether you'd show. He is not easy to chart and you have never been good at dealing with what you can t name.

The door opens after three knocks. He doesn't seem surprised to see you, his greeting a wordless nod of the head, his lips dry as they graze the sides of your cheeks. He smells like iron flakes and other minerals, coarse, elemental. Praquin hasn't folded up the futon and you note that the sheets still hold a slight fold. This tells you his sleep is peaceful.

The tentative beams filtering through the window promise heat; the day would be warm if it had the heart. He offers you stale bread he's toasted in the small corner oven, real butter melting, apricot jam and a bowl of steamed milk with coffee. You ask for some sugar please but he says *non, cela to fera grossir,* that will make you fat, so you drink it and complain silently about the bitterness but don't move a hand in the direction of the sugar cubes.

He watches you from across the table, calculating, evaluating.

Then his hand darts out, eel-like, and pulls your palm away from the steamy side of the ceramic milk bowl and you feel uneasy.

His fingers are rough, their tips callused and his knuckles are cracked, perhaps from the drawing power of clay. He turns your hand over, running his fingers along its lines and grooves. He stops at your wrists, rubs the nude underside.

—*Belles mains,* You have beautiful hands, he says as he releases them.

The compliment cannot be authentic, your nails are broken and the surrounding skin inflamed (if you would just quit biting them), and you wonder what he was really looking for. You retract your arms from the table and slide your hands under your thighs.

Removing your clothes is not the hardest part. That comes when he asks that you put your hair up so that nothing falls over your shoulders. It is this that feels like a pulling back, a shell removed. You also have developed a slouch, hunched as if wounded. He wants you to sit straight.

—*Pendant combien de temps,* for how long? you ask.

—*Tant que je to le dis,* he replies. For as long as I say.

Chapter thirteen

The pale, saffron light breaking through the old glass offers no balm for the goosebumps that rise on your arms, big as welts along your legs. You are bent sidewinder-like, holding a pose, wrapped in a white sheet as if in tissue paper for so many minutes you have stopped counting. Your feet are blocks of ice, you're sure of that.

—*Monsieur,* you begin, certain he'll be annoyed, *Monsieur, j'ai froid.* In France, one, that is to say, a person, has cold, as if it is a form of ownership. One also has age, has fear, has thirst. This construction has never felt accurate to you, the same even in Spanish, *Tengo hambre, I* have hunger. So much more accurate in the English to say, I am these things; cold and fear are a state of being. How much more elastic the English language can be; you have come to appreciate the way it accommodates invention, how it always finds a few more beats.

Praquin sniffs, doesn't answer, and you think he might not have heard you. You know how hearing closes in concentration, when there's nothing but the roar of your own blood in your ears to fill the space between thoughts.

—*Monsieur?* you ask again.

—Jean, he corrects.

His hands continue their march over the silt-colored lump in front of him, oblivious to the temperature.

—Okay, Jean. Jean, you say, jerking your head around to accentuate the point. *Jai froid. Vous m'entendez?* I'm cold, get it?

—*Merde.* His hands fall from the clay. *Bouge pas. Tu m'ecoutes, toi? I* told you not to move.

Instantly you regret it. You're a series of junctions, after all, nothing but planes and dimensions, proportion, texture. You want to say, Sorry, but a man you once slept with told you Americans say they're sorry too much and everybody knows they're not. Come to think of it, that's probably true.

You return to the serpentine, contrite. Watch your breath coil through the chilly air toward the narrow, long mirror. It leans against the wall just so, to catch all angles.

—*Pas jolie,* Praquin snorts, as if reading your mind. It can't be said you're pretty. His eyes meet yours in the reflection of the glass. One might say you are... interesting.

You look away. He is not lying. You are not beautiful but you do seem rare, irregular enough to draw the eye, one part placed unexpectedly next to the other. The faint olive cast of your skin and very light eyes, the one point you can identify as inherited from your mother. Hair, an undefined series of browns, falling in a snarl of corkscrew curls. People will often say, Where did you get all that hair, girl?

You really have no clue who gave it to you.

I am thinking how the rank smell of menthol cigarettes clung to the quilt fibres on her bed. The air carried powder and the hot, boozy scent of Tabu cologne, the thick smell of reheated coffee. She was bending over the porcelain sink in the bathroom, getting close enough to the mirror to put on liner evenly, making a wet, black-whipped crescent over each eye. Next she rounded her lips and fashioned a sort of bow with lipstick. Its color was called *rose du printemps* and I told her that meant Spring Rose.

—My daughter the genius, she said and winked at me, carefully, so as not to smudge the liner. Her breath coated the glass with translucent clouds, her beauty always a kind of shrapnel that explodes in your face.

—Who is my dad? I said, out of nowhere. I didn't know I was thinking about that until I heard myself say the words.

She didn't answer for a moment, then said, Hand me my cigs, there, on the bed.

She has this way of flipping her lighter open with a snap of her wrist.

We waited, silent, for the flint to spark, anticipating the cherry glow of the drag.

—Nick, she said. That's who you love. That's who loves you.

—Come on. Tell me about my real father.

—What's there to tell? she said, ditching the lighter. Shit. Where are the matches?

—What do you remember about him?

—He was a great dancer, she said, feeling around the shelves in the bathroom for a matchbook. And then left me to collect the pieces. Do you get it?

—What else? I asked her. I would not stop until I had the details. Did he play sports? Did he pray to God? Did he ever, ever, make her laugh?

—What else? Who the hell knows what else. I knew him a week.

The match lighting her cigarette erupted in tangerine flame, putting light in the tracks around her eyes. She exhaled through her nose.

—He held his fork upside down. He never put his knife down when he ate. I thought that was so suave, she said. He told me he lived in Mexico City, but his family was from Italy. Or something like that. Very European.

She said the trouble all started when she wore a red crepe wool dress, three-quarter length with spaghetti straps. She said, Nothing looks better on a blonde than red.

There was the smell of pipe tobacco smoke on him, fine bones in his wrist, the tailored stitch of his collar. I imagine she had Cleopatra eyes and smelled like the kind of woman who turns faithless and wanders.

And then there was me. She waited until I was six months old before she took me out in public, dressed in a lemon-colored cotton jumper, a bow taped to my head. Our first outing was to the grocery store.

—We walked in and words ended mid-syllable, she said. I think those Boston bitches wanted me to just fall off the end of the earth.

—No one said anything to you? I asked her, thinking I could never understand the picture the two of us created there in that store, my fat baby hands grasping at her platinum hair, my wet mouth gumming what I could grab.

—We got maybe one hello from the guy at the meat counter, she said. God, how I wish we'd had Nick then. He would have made heads roll had anybody looked at us sideways, you just know it.

She returned to the mirror. Another coat of liner.

* * *

Praquin is talking as you dress, no screen for modesty, just the high back of a chair to balance against.

—*Tu sais, Sabine, tu pourrais être française. Quand on voit la profondeur du regard que tu as,* he tells you as he comes to stand near.

What does this mean, that you could have been French? Then it comes to you that, of course, this is a compliment, the nicest thing he can imagine saying. You pull on your shirt and tell him, Who knows? Maybe I am.

Chapter fourteen

McDonald's is a kind of touchstone, the orange and yellow unique to its interior soothes me. I realize this indicates an inherent weakness, so I admit my trips there to no one. Not that I have anyone to tell.

I am used to seeing other Americans skating through this culture on their Eurorail passes, but the one in line next to me hooks my attention. He's been standing there for at least five minutes. I could go ahead of him but then I would miss the careful way his eyes read each menu line, as if he's trying to decipher any words that translate as "fries" and "vanilla shake". If he knew how his red-tagged Levis, his white basketball shoes with the stripe at the heel make him look garish and unformed in this country, so raw, would he still wear them? Yes. I can tell by the hard lines around his mouth. If it were not for the worn sweatshirt so typically American, I might have wondered if he were a Basque separatist, maybe an Andalusian who wanted to fight bulls, but who found when the moment came that he lacked the red and black it takes to be a matador.

A cap of dark hair frames his face. Sandalwood eyes, heavy at the bottom rim, as if he were born knowing that things would always end badly. Black lashes, elaborate as lace. He studies the menu board and there is a crease between his eyes. His knuckles are bony. He seems like the kind of man who will smell faintly of motor oil and gasoline, his breath like the sugary garnet rings made by port wine in a glass. His skin is a caramel that seems as if it would stick to my fingers. *Beau mec,* Madame Doumic would say, in those two words dismissing him. Such a good-looking man is better left on the shelf, a Frenchwoman believes. Any man so physically compelling must be severely flawed in other, fundamental ways, because Nature is never that bountiful.

Now he's actually made it through his order, and the cashier tells him *quarante-huit francs.* He fumbles through the currency wadded in his hand, and I know, because I too have done this, that he is stalling, the bills are unfamiliar, he needs time to interpret how much the total is. He must be flustered and has forgotten to look at the register, where the digital numbers appear plainly.

I lean forward.

—Forty-eight francs, I tell him quietly. He snaps his head around to look at me, his smile seems to spread across half his face. One incisor has a small chip.

—*Merci,* he says, and his voice is lush, the kind that can make a woman cry for no reason at all. *Merci,* he repeats. His guidebook must have offered useful phrases. He hands the money to the cashier, who is unimpressed.

—*Parlez-vous anglais?* he asks me boldly, practised to the point of sounding fluent, barely a trace of accent. This is spoken as if he has a contingency plan if I say no, I don't speak English. But he's used up two of the classic travel phrases, and I figure he can't have practised that many more.

—*Oui. Couramment,* I reply, though I would bet money he doesn't know the word for "fluently". I turn to the cashier and order curtly, *Un grand Coca. C'est tout.* I try to sound like ordering is an inconvenience I suffer only because of thirst, not because I really long for the burning carbonation of a Coke.

The man stands beside me holding his tray with its pile of fries and assorted meats wrapped in colored papers, grease spotting through. He seems to want to say something more. As I get the Coke from the counter I turn to look into his eyes and smile before moving toward the door, but he follows me.

—Thank you again, he says, speaking slowly with the kind of proper diction appropriate for addressing people unused to speaking a language. It occurs to me he must think I'm French.

—Would you like to join me, if you have a minute? he asks, gesturing with his tray toward the molded plastic booth.

I still the reflex to laugh at this colossal miscalculation on his part, this foolishness, and instead I just nod. Sure.

He extends a hand. My name's Abe.

He doesn't look like he goes with the name Abe, as in Lincoln, as in stalwart and severe, as in old-fashioned principles. He has the look of someone who doesn't ride the brakes on a curve, the kind of person who says, Who cares? Why bother? *Arriba chica,* we'll miss the party.

—*Enchanté,* I say, finally shaking his hand with a brief grasp. You are American?

—American? he replies. Sure. Star and stripes forever.

I sit across from him on the swivel seat at the yellow formica table. The moment is awkward. He reads the wallpaper meant to look like books lining shelves, examines the plastic bust of Voltaire in the corner. I consider what it means to be mistaken for French and Praquin's comment. The clues to what I am are on me, just like his shoes, but obviously his eye isn't trained. Yet, perhaps it's not that at all; I know that need to talk to someone who is part of this city, who can transform it beyond the precise green of gardens and crowded *terrasses,* beyond palaces built for Charlemagne and the blanched bricks and the small cars infesting the streets with traffic. If he realized I was an American the allure he now finds would evaporate, and why not enjoy this moment?

—Why don't you eat in a French restaurant? I say in the way of a question, but mimic exactly that insinuation of reprimand I have heard so often.

He observes me, a fry pinched between his fingers, and it occurs to me he might become defensive in the face of Gallic superiority.

—My dad always said "Buy American", he says in a mock whisper, pretending a confidence. Besides, I really do like hamburgers.

He leans forward, his eyebrow raised. What, may I ask, are you doing here?

I shrug, ignore the question, tell him, Let me recommend a good place, not too expensive, bringing a pen out of my purse to write the address of Le Mouton Enragé on the paper place-mat. His eyes never leave my face and I think, what are the possibilities? Do I tell him he makes me think of the sweet smell of burning piñon, will he say I am someone he will not forget, will he feel the heat that burns me up, will he know how to keep a secret?

Then you become aware of how your jean button now pinches your waist as you sit. The truth is you have no right to pretend there's enough time in the world for an evening that will lead nowhere and, God, haven't you done this too often before, as if you were simply a girl with nothing to untangle? Maybe the others could be written down as an exercise or a balm or just as practice, but what could be the reason for this one, other than he has temporarily lost his bearings and you just happened along, a marker in the road. This time that will not be enough.

I stand abruptly and his expression dims.

—I have to go, I tell him. I have other things I need to do.

—Maybe I'll see you at this restaurant sometime? He holds out the paper I just handed him, examines the words written on it. How would you say this? Mow-tun En-Rage?

His laugh is self-deprecating and it makes me smile. I cover my mouth with the back of my hand because French women never show this much tooth.

—Close enough, I tell him, reminding myself that men like this are a mirage that dissipate the closer you get. I start walking. But I resist breaking the thread of contact.

—Just don't order anything called *boudin noir,* I say quickly. They'll tell you it's good, but they lie.

—Boo-dan? What is that?

—Pig's blood sausage.

—You've got to be kidding, he says, making a face. I see the relaxed way he leans back into the plastic chair, comfortable with the space he takes up. What else do they eat here?

—Anything that doesn't keep up, I tell him, but I am heading out the exit. Perhaps my reply didn't reach him, camouflaged by the noise of the street.

Chapter fifteen

I am perfecting the skill of watching the world behind the tabloid pages of *Libé*, only my eyes periscope above the edge as I survey the passing crowds in the metro at Odéon. The evidence suggests that populations are like turf, every blade individual yet so similar to the next in height and girth that the most remarkable feature appears to be one's likeness to the next.

When my eye lands on the exception to this even sameness it surprises like a kind of static electricity. It takes a second to put the particulars into focus, but it is indeed Abe. From the opposite platform I can see him jump the metal banister. Good man. I never buy metro tickets, either. The easy way he swings his arms, tucking his legs, conjures an idea of melody, how unencumbered a human can be. I wonder where he is going, if he is the kind of person who needs to have a destination, if it doesn't bother him to have to ask for directions.

The train comes and the human lattice of people boarding and unboarding thickens. I strain to catch sight of him but lose him in the weave. The hydraulic hiss of the train door closing means I am missing the train. That's Alright. Sometimes I come here just to sit and read, as if I'm going on a long trip. Waiting is the most salient part of going anywhere.

*   *   *

I scan the pages for stories about America, because they always seem to be about a place I don't know, an ominous black wave swelling somewhere on the other side of the Atlantic. There is a new president, George Bush. It would have been my first election, had I gone to the embassy to vote, but there was something more pressing that day. Perhaps I was in class. Perhaps I was at that brasserie with the man who said he played pro soccer when he wasn't working as a *petit fonctionnaire* at the post office.

My eyes land on an article about something called RU 487, a pill. I understand trials are beginning. Women who want to end their pregnancies take it like a vitamin in the morning and spend the day cramped on the toilet. Blood can be measured in a cup. A black mass appears. Complaints of a bad headache, nausea, the possibility of a few days off work. Questions about reliability, several report side effects.

I put the paper down.

Another train comes. Another train leaves.

And what if you should, on that morning as you rise, notice that the rain has stopped. The streets appear waxed, a sudden sheen covers the worn stones. What if you ignore the fact that the heavy bellies of the ever-present clouds bow, hanging still as if at any moment they could tear, pouring down.

Nick said this: It's better to regret something you did than something you didn't do.

Chapter sixteen

I am thinking about that American. His voice, it was convincing, the way men talk to cats in unguarded moments. The curve of his black hair, as if I could put my hands through it and sink up to my elbows, thinking, finally, I have found the color of night.

It was that summer, going all the way north to Artesia to fix a roof on a barn for one of his cousins. Although you were only fourteen you drove the truck with "Navarro Construction and Audio Equipment" painted in red block letters across the hood. Driving through the singed heart of the *llano* Nick turned up the radio, said, This song here by Dave Brubeck is the first ever in five-four to reach the charts. Maybe the only. Hear it? One-two-three-four-FIVE, one-two-three-four-FIVE. That's cool, *que no?*

And he played along, batting at space, his hands moving like sticks. On the cab seat sat a six-pack of yellow-bottled Coronas, two empty. Nick held a third between his legs, drank by pushing his tongue up against the opening like a stopper, then releasing. Beer poured down his throat in one even stream. When the bottle was half empty he looked over at you, said, *Cerveza?* When you shook your head no he said, Good girl.

When the truck arrived at the property you turned off the engine and moved to open the door, but he spread his hand over your shoulder.

—Let's just sit here a while, *hijita,* he said. Enjoy the view. Take it easy.

You followed his gaze past the window into a leafy field of alfalfa, its violet hue and a scent sweet like that of young girls and horses. He focused on the tall iron sprinklers spaced in the field every few feet, forcing a spray of white mist out in an arc. He held his fingers to his lips. Listen, he said. Shug-shug-SHUG, shug-shug-SHUG, from the sprinklers there?

There was lunch. Baloney and cheese rolled in a flour tortilla with green chile. That far out on the highway no radio signals reached the antennae, so Nick read a chapter from *Zilltron 2000,* one of the space-alien paperbacks he always had with him. He told you of event horizons around black holes, the points of endless density where nothing can escape. He looked up to point to the Guadalupe Mountains in the distance.

—No doubt the government spooks have those hills hollowed out by now, he said.

—If they're hollow how do they stand up?

—Titanium warheads. He sounded sure. That's the kind of thing that happens all the time in the military. I seen some things there's no explaining.

As he talked he fingered the long scar running in a crescent from the ridge of his right temple to the corner of his mouth, how it looked sucked in and greedy pulling at the evenness of his face, the way alluvial fans grab soil from mountainsides and pour it onto the desert basin as so much dust.

—How'd you get that? you pointed to his face.

—This? Some gig. The Lamplighter, over in El Paso, he said. Your mom sewed me up.

—Is that when you met? In the hospital?

He laughed. Yeah, but it was a parking-lot more like. I was cut up. She said she could fix me up, so I let her.

He remembered how she stood in front of him with her back to the moon so high in the sky it threw shadows on clouds, stars like polished silver dollars strewn in a trail leading too far. (Her bleached hair would have been made sterling in reflection.) As he lay in the back seat of the car he could see through the window a world in black and white, the cool light cast across the desert creating a shining haematite, a pasture's barbed wire looking like strings of crystal to him. He told her she was the most beautiful thing he had ever seen. She said, It's just a trick of the night.

I have no idea how long I have been sitting at this station. I have to admit a certain seduction, an attraction to the curve of the shiny buttercup tiles, the way chrome from the trains throws brightness across their glazed surface.

When they ask me why I didn't finish school I will tell them I have this, and that I know the tense, flushed glinn of morning, the humid days pressing across the window panes. This will have to be enough.

Thursday

Chapter seventeen

Praquin wants you to talk this morning, says tell him a story. *Raconte-moi une petite histoire. On a besoin de quelquechose de léger.*

—I don't know any funny little stories, you tell him. Your back is towards him again, your head turned in profile. You do not look at him. It is easier this way. Today he is almost giddy with cheerfulness and on him the emotion seems grotesque, a malformation.

This doesn't seem to dampen his enthusiasm. Instead he wants now to discuss what you study in school.

—*La littérature,* you say. Although this is a lie it is less cumbersome than the truth (how often that is the case). Anyhow, that was always the dream, to come here and study literature, because even from your high-school text books the sound of poetry rose, narcotic, to be inhaled. But the Lions' Club is a white-collar professional organization. This is an exchange-type deal, and what they had to offer was a round-trip ticket, a living stipend and tuition paid for a one-year program in "mass communications", what translates as a trade school for French youths who don't have time for things that won't get them a job. This program might mean a post at a radio

station or a secretarial position at *Le Monde,* if they are very, very
lucky. In retrospect this was the first clue the reality would be very
different from the fantasy; you hid the twinge of disappointment
behind extreme exuberance, *Thank you, thank you, this means so much.*
Disappointment should not be construed as ingratitude. Think of the
French student who ended up at the Dona Ana Community College
in Las Cruces. Besides, you told yourself you could always read the
poems on your own but in all honesty you haven't read one since the
day you landed at Charles de Gaulle. *Oui. La littérature.*

—*C'est bien,* he enthuses. How happy this makes him. And
of course here come the questions, what have you learned, what are
you studying at the moment? This could be a dangerous path because
you could give the wrong answer and then this construction would
topple like wooden blocks. Stop the process by asking who was his
favorite poet when he studied these things at the university?

Nod your head and make little affirmative sounds as he
expounds on the deceptive simplicity of Ponge, the transcendent
nature of Camus.

—*J'ai toujours admiré Apollinaire,* he mentions in passing. Suddenly you're paying attention, brighten at the prospect of sharing
something you love: "Le Pont Mirabeau" by Apollinaire was the first
poem you learnt by heart. Miss Ortiz had warned it was a difficult
choice for a first-year student, the other classmates had no interest in
getting beyond "Frère Jacques". You struggled to decode the words,
they said something about emotion flowing like the water under a
bridge, love passing and pain staying but joy always returning. You
got that much right off. Still, there was so much buried within the
structure you had to pry each new understanding from it. Finally,
how it glided, felt almost like singing.

So now the words come to as easily as your own name. You
begin to say them out loud because you think he will appreciate the
time it took to learn them.

Sous le pont Mirabeau coule la Seine
Et nos amours
Faut-il qu'il m'en souvienne

La joie venait toujours après la peine.

Praquin moves to close the few feet separating the two of you, standing at your back. His hands are cold, encrusted, and he rubs a knuckle along the length of your arm, pressing into its softness. He touches your hair, his blunt fingers petting the long strands, making them stick together.

—*Monsieur?* you ask, not knowing what is safe, when to move, how to calculate the circumstance now being created. *Qu'est-ce que vous voulez?* What do you want?

—*C'est dommage,* he says in a way that prickles the hair on the back of your neck.

—*C'est quoi, dommage?* What's a shame? You think you have made some mistake in the recitation, mentally go back over the words to see where you could have faltered. You straighten, swivel to look at him squarely.

Instantly you regret it.

His eyes are fixed on the swell of your buttocks and his pants are open, his hand clamped around his penis, the wrinkled hood. He tugs in strangling bursts, his face puckered as if to suck venom. Quickly you turn your head back toward the wall and will your heart to stop pounding so loud, like a bird dumbly throwing itself against a window. If you're very quiet and think about something else, maybe this won't be happening, but then his voice comes up from behind you.

—*Continues. Parles-moi encore,* speak to me again.

You think about a bird, but you need to have hollow bones for flight. You could stand up now and demand the money you've earned but what if he decided not to give it to you? The police would want to know what you were doing without your clothes, why you were working without a permit. They might want to take you in, maybe you wouldn't be out by Monday and there is no second chance. You would be caged for as long as you could stand to live.

You consider this: It's just a matter of seconds and this too will be finished. He has a need, that is all. You begin slowly, trying for neutral tones. *Sous le pont Mirabeau.*

He makes a sound that could be a yelp, like touching a burner. Then there is a thread of wet down your back. You bite the inside of your cheek and keep yourself quiet.

He clears his throat, pulls the sheet up to wipe your skin.

—*Cést dommage que tu perdes ton p'tit accent américain. Je le trouve charmant.* It's a shame you're losing your little American accent. I find it so charming.

Chapter eighteen

There is no clock on the wall but the length of the shadows draping the corners tell you that this day is finally shifting into afternoon. And still you sit.

—*Monsieur?* Jean? *Il se fait tard.* It's getting late.

—*Qu'est-ce que tu veux dire?* What are you trying to say?

It seems I have been trying to say so many things for such a long time. Now he asks me, and I don't know which response to give. Perhaps I will say, when I shut my eyes there is the acute sunlight, and the drying amber tips of grasses, and those mesas no more than thin blue threads against a panorama so vast as to be at times unholy. I feel shut in in this city composed of so many bricks and worn by the rubbing of so many bodies in its streets. I want to explain that the perpetual clouds suspended over Paris diffuse and ease all points of light, adding luminescence where none otherwise would arise.

I know this too will end, and soon, and I have no more answers than before. I can't reconcile how this quiet, mannered way of living, the desire for fresh flowers in a room no matter its modest size, can be any use whatsoever in surviving the rest of my life. I am considering that wall-to-wall carpeting and a paycheque every two weeks may not be the form of pathetic consolation prize I once thought, but a bedrock that covers a void too deep to see bottom.

I believed French would cover me with civilization, a protective coating, a kind of mantle I could wear for the rest of my life. But, now I understand language is not a goal but a means, and I have begun to imagine the day when it will be as if my mouth never formed these words, when they will not come to me like breathing. One day I will retrieve the words in a halting speech, but I will not be flustered in the least, because I simply will not care. The structure of all language will be known to me, how it is conjured from the human brain. One will have no particular value over the next.

Perhaps what I am trying to say is that exhaustion is often mistaken for confidence.

I understand the feeling of exile, that every individual voice creates a sound that exists nowhere else in the universe. I now realize that all those years Nick was telling everyone he would eventually take his elk hunting rifle out to the barn, and nothing would have stopped my mother from going out there when she heard the sound, and what I mean by this is I am not the cause of people acting in deadly and unmanageable ways. I must believe that I bear witness and nothing more.

Perhaps what I am trying to say is this: Let me tell you about the world I had to make from that. Let me tell you about disintegration and how to remain standing when you can't trust the ground beneath your feet. I mean that I cannot tie everything together, and what to do with all these pieces? I have been listening to everyone in the hope that I might hear how life can be lived and that someone can tell me that they know how to make it Alright. That is no longer necessary. I have divined that there are never any guarantees and that everyone flies without a net.

—*Ça va,* Sabine? How are you doing?

Rather than a gentle asking of how you are, this is a directive, more rightly said, You will do Alright, Sabine. Your name sounds awkward when he says it, too long, an exaggeration.

—Bean, *s'il vous plaît. C'est mon surnom.* Bean is my nickname.

He makes no comment, you hear only the squeak and rustle as he moves, his muttering breath. You turn around and see he is wiping off his hands. It was an idle question, forgotten once asked.

—*C'est belge,* you say on impulse. It's Belgian, did you know that?

Praquin turns his head and juts his chin forward as he shrugs, which means, so what are you talking about?

—Sabine, *mon nom,* Sabine, is common among the Belgian, you say with conviction although this is a complete fabrication. I got it from my father. You remember my Belgian father? *Mon père, vous vous souvenez de mon père belge?*

He is looking straight into your eyes. It's true that in this culture people often have a direct gaze, but it is not the kind of sight that takes a sum total but rather it is an atomization, the breaking into parts.

—*Oui. Ça y est. Habille-toi.* I've got it, so get dressed.

You go to the chair where you have folded your clothes. The pointed ache of each breast makes the move uncomfortable and reminds you that Monday is the reason for all this. Your underwear is so cold it feels wet and you think, maybe it could be, so you wring it in your hands. No. It's dry. Ever since you found out you have more than the flu (how sick it makes you feel), you've been seized periodically with the possibility that blood will unexpectedly gush down your leg and you will have no way to catch it or hide it, and blood is difficult to clean up, its many shades of purple deteriorate to rust. The way it dyes cloth fibres, the way, months afterwards, fine spots turn up on things no one thought to wipe off.

—Sabine? His voice is softer. You stiffen.

—*Oui?*

—*Ne change pas ta coiffure pour demain.* Don't change your hair tomorrow.

He returns to wiping his hands, runs the ridge of one nail under the ridge of another on his left hand to clean the brown line from it and then brings it to his nose, inhaling briefly.

You hurry to get the rest of your clothes.

Chapter nineteen

At first it was as if my memory of him had been obliterated. I could not recall even the color of his eyes, I could not hear the sound of his voice. But something has changed. More and more his words come to me, as if he were speaking them for the first time.

—You're trying to aim that shotgun like it's a rifle, *corazon*, Nick said. You can't aim a shotgun. You got to just point the gun and let your eye lead to the bird.

—Right.

—Put the stock up to your shoulder when I say "pull". Then, just eye that son of a bitch and slap the trigger.

—Right.

When he said "pull" I did as I was told. I had the butt lodged right against the cup of my shoulder. But as my eye followed the clay bird I lifted my cheek away from the barrel and couldn't control the recoil. The barrel's worn metal slammed against my cheek, there was the crack of my head against the dirt, and then Nick was giving me a hand up. He was there so fast he must have run.

—Are you okay? He reached to touch my face but I pulled back. Holy fuck, that'll be a shiner.

—Did I break the clay?

—That gun's too big for you, *hija*. You don't need a sixteen-gauge.

—I like the gun fine. I'm okay.

He shook his head. Your mother's going to have my ass.

—I'll tell her I fell.

—Tell her whatever, but you're not shooting that gun again, he said. He was starting to pick up the targets.

—Nick?

—What?

—Did I break the clay?

He took a minute to answer, his eyes searching the ground for spare ammo dropped by mistake.

—Next time, he said. Next time you'll do it.

And if I were to have known a father, what would have been different?

Chapter twenty

Madame Doumic said she wanted to have dinner but in reality this meal is yet another test. There is a way each cheese must be sliced, and I do not know how it is supposed to be done. I remember horizontal for the Roquefort, vertical for the Brie, but about the rest I have no idea, even though she taught me this early on through a series of dinners my first week in Paris. She said it was to help me settle in but I also understood the other goal of observing the gaps in the seams of my education.

I go ahead and slice the Camembert on the diagonal. There is an audible pause. Madame Doumic shakes her head, seems wrung out by my ignorance.

—*Laisse-moi faire,* Let me do it. *Fais attention, ma fille.*

I pass the platter into her hands, twisted as the roots of these city trees pushing through concrete. She slices thinly along the outside edge and puts the morsel on my plate as if it is all one movement.

—*Evidement les fromages n'existent pas aux Etats Unis,* Evidently there is no cheese in the United States.

—*Si,* I object weakly. There is cheese, just not this kind.

Her expression is pleasant, she lifts her knife gracefully above the plate.

—That is not cheese, my dear. *C'est du plastique.* It's practically plastic.

I know that for her America is all the Wild West and Trigger, and maybe there is something to that. Mia and I did shoot rats at the dump, exploding them against trash bags and old bed-springs, and we did race our ponies in the arroyo that one summer when we built a fort in the cottonwoods and spied on Robbie Taffoya kissing boys in the pecan orchard next door. How the verdant boughs arched against the sun. This makes me think of homemade tamales, golden masa toasted and steaming, the burn of chile, the not wanting to brush my teeth.

I begin to tell her about this but I don't know the vocabulary, something is lost in translation, the French words won't hold chile verde and open flame. I try to explain it anyway, and it could be said my descriptions are accurate, in a textbook way. She comments on this, how she's noticed my accent is so different from most American voices she encounters.

—I grew up with Spanish, I tell her, meaning that accent is a process of learning to hear, how finely attuned the ear can become with practice.

—*Bien entendu,* of course, *pour parler aux domestiques, comme je parle portugais,* she says, thinking I speak Spanish for the same reason she speaks Portuguese, to tell the maid what to do.

She says this in such a way that I can hear my grandmother on the phone, saying, Do you think Jackie Kennedy speaks Spic? Christ no. French at least will get you somewhere.

I thought I knew what she meant.

I see Nick standing past a fog of nicotine and the polished glare off the bar, the 1985 Farm 'n' Feed calendar still on the wall and a signed poster of the St Pauli Girls over the cash register. Two sweating Tecates were clasped in the knotty fingers of one hand, the other held his chin as he listened to a customer complain that peace had killed all the maintenance jobs at the missile range over in Alamogordo, that women from Albuquerque are too mean and most of them have been to school. Nick's eyes were clear, a series of brown shades. He thought he caught a glimpse of my mother and the possibility straightened him. But when he saw it was just me wearing her coat, his shoulders bent once again.

    —*¿Que pasa, chica?*
    —*Nada de particular.*

Madame Doumic is telling me I should meet some nice French people my own age. She says, Why don't you and Pascale go out, enjoy yourselves, have *quelque chose à boire?*

    I shrug. It's not so easy.

    —It's as easy as you make it, she says.

    I rub my fingers together as if I'm pinching salt, the symbol for no money.

    She smiles, says, two attractive young women need only to look nice to have a good time. You never know who you might meet, she says. And I wonder at the world she once knew before time eroded her body, swelled her joints painfully.

Chapter twenty-one

The night air clings, wraps me in a faint sweetness. Spice cupboard, cinnamon, the pinch of ginger. In honour of the break in the clouds I am wearing my one good dress, black with fake pearl buttons lined ant-like up the front. Humidity wraps around me as a kind of shawl, the slick feel of my thighs oiled after my bath rubbing at the top as I walk. I've pulled my hair up in a loose configuration, but strands stick to the back of my neck; I notice this as I pull errant curls behind my ear, finger the silver hoop at my lobe.

Tonight my only plan had been to stay in and watch *Deux Flics à Miami*, which I would never do if it were in English and still *Miami Vice*. But Madame Doumic was insistent I ask Pascale to join me out for a drink, and though at first I resisted (we have never before even crossed the street at the same time) Madame Doumic had started to pry. *Alors, pourquoi tu fais la gueule,* so why are you moping about?

That is how we have come to walk side by side to the bar behind the Panthéon.

Pascale surprised me by asking only one question. *Où est-ce qu'on va?* Where are we going? I said, I know a bar. I told myself I'll just leave if I don't like it.

But I like it. Wood walls, a Pittsburgh Steelers banner, Motown sounding reedy and thin off a cassette player and even the crackling speakers in the corner sounding fresh and I think, everything translates as new. Every bar everywhere must have the same yeasty-sticky floors, gripping your shoes, keeping you grounded. No one is going to slide off the Earth here, that's for sure (Mom always said that about the tiles in Nick's bar). People threading their way through, back-to-back, an arm presses into my waist and then moves. Voices in French, German, one might be Chinese. So many different people. This must be the sound of speaking in tongues.

Pascale stands next to me. Her wide, red mouth. She sings along to the music, *Mustang Polly, you batter show that mustang down.* Although she carries the tune her mistakes are a kind of high-frequency sonic torture, so I stop her, explain what she is singing, why it makes no sense. She actually laughs at herself, wants to practise the lyrics, tells me to say them first, then she'll repeat. Then I'm laughing too, it's like meeting her for the first time and liking her. I feel air fill my lungs and realize, for all these months I must have been holding my breath. The couple next to us doesn't understand when we talk American and that makes us talk louder.

Pascale nudges me with her elbow. *Un fan. Sois cool,* she says, as if telling a secret, leans in, like reading a menu over my shoulder.

I follow her gaze to the corner of the bar and there is a man with skinny arms hunched on a stool. He studies me with a lopsided smile. When he realizes I'm looking at him his smile stretches wider and he mouths the words, *Salut, ma gonzesse,* Hey there, chick.

—*C'est pas sérieux, ça,* I tell Pascale. This guy can't be serious. I say, maybe he's talking to you, but she shakes her head, No. It's you.

And he laughs, as if he has just invented something new and invigorating, as if he thinks, how unfortunate her mind can't understand my brilliance.

All at once adrenaline spikes up my spine, straightening my

shoulders, the tilt of my head just so. Blood is beating in my temples and it's been a long, long time since I hit anything.

When I first arrived with my American sheen I was eager for any kindness, any crack in the door, and these kind of scrawny men, some even in suits and ties, would say such vile and unimaginative things and because I didn't know the vocabulary yet I would just smile politely and turn my eyes down and end up having dinner with them. And then more. This was a temporary shelter of sorts but now it has been long enough, and I have learned. I stare back at this man with a look that says I recognize him as the face of an otherwise nameless plague.

—*Il est nul,* I say to Pascale but I keep my face turned toward the man so he can read my lips. I motion to her, let's go stand over there. We start to walk and then I feel a sharp twinge at my scalp; my hair has just been pulled. I turn and the lopsided man is putting a wiry strand of my hair in his shirt pocket, trying to take a part of me on the sly.

I stand in front of him. The musk of a sweating, unwashed man reaches my nose and I have the urge to gag. I move quickly to reclaim the hairs he's just tucked into his shirt, but his reflexes are rapid and unexpectedly strong and he holds my hand there against his chest. Bony. His heart beats one-two-one-twoone, the pounding so even for a moment I imagine it is in my hands. And it makes me think of the first time I shot a gun, the click and slide, warm, like a burner, the itch of lead all over, the pop, the bang, the sound of someone making up his mind.

—*Qu'est-ce que tu fous là, toi?* What are you doing? he squeals, a mouse in a grain bin, the kind that bites your hand even though you're only trying to shoo it away.

—*Ce sont les miennes. Tu n'as pas le droit.* Those are mine, you don't have the right. I say this slowly, accent exaggerated. It occurs to me he thinks he's being amusing. This charade is somehow intended to charm. I pull my hand away but the residue remains and maybe I should just go wash it off.

—*C'est des vrais?* Look at this stuff, he says, I just wanted to see the hair was for real.

How often has it been said. What do you do with all that curly hair? I let it grow long because no one knows how to cut it.

But what am I doing, still standing in front of this guy.

—*Ecoute connard. Ne me retouche pas,* Don't touch me again asshole, I tell him, my voice heavy. I walk alone to the other side of the bar.

Suddenly I feel deflated and look around for Pascale, but she is nowhere to be found.

—Pascale? I call, looking through the crowd until I see the crown of her dark head, bent in conversation with a cluster of other French people, some look vaguely familiar, as if they might be from school.

—Pascale? I call out again, more to myself this time because I understand a reply won't come. I miss the sound of another woman's laughter when there are no men around. I would have liked to know a friend somewhere in this country, but I am not unhappy. I know how to be alone in a bar.

I was no more than eight when I followed the waves of steel-string guitar and electric bass coming from up the river. Rudy Gabaldon and the Boomchaca Band were just warming up, and I wanted to catch their first set, when they played "Wildthing" in Spanish.

Mom put me to bed instead.

—Goodnight, goodnight, she sang softly. The bedtime ritual was for me to call back, Don't let the begbugs bite, but I pouted and stayed silent.

She closed the door, but the hall light spread out from the gap underneath it. I waited for the coughing ignition, the crunching sound of tires to tell me she had left for the bar. Then I followed, stumbling on the driveway gravel in front of the house, sharp granite pebbles always finding the most tender point in the arch of my foot. I remember the mustard splash of sulphur earth exposed on the grated roadway. I walked toward the pink neon "On Tap" sign, shimmering in the heat like rainbow trout scales in water.

I sit at the corner of the bar near two men bent toward each other discussing President Mitterand's prostate cancer, scarves wrapped at their throats as if they live in fear of catching a chill. They drink tequila as if it is a form of sweet liqueur, or like putting their dry lips to tea.

The bartender walks slowly toward me, reluctance around him like a shield.

—*Vous désirez?* What would you like? he says, as if I were any other customer. The problem is we have no word to describe each other. Not lover. Not acquaintance. Each presumes a domesticated knowledge of the other we do not have. I want to tell him, beyond the initial contact I felt nothing but a fever to leave, I am not the kind of woman who forms attachments or affection easily.

I tell him I'll have what the two men next to me are having. *Ils ne savent pas comment le faire,* I say, They don't know how to do it.

The bartender nods, says, The booze of your people, I recall.

He doesn't understand New Mexico is part of the United States, but then, neither do some Americans. I give up and agree. *Soy una de la gente,* I tell him in Spanish. I'm one of the people.

He produces two shot glasses and a bottle of tequila, clear, the look no different than spring water.

—Blue agave, I nod approvingly. *Mira,* I tell him again in Spanish. Watch. Tequila requires ceremony and flourish. Salt, tequila, lime. Lick, sip, suck. That's how it goes.

The alcohol hits my throat and it feels good, automatic. The man who pulled my hair stays at the other end of the bar's length but still he watches. I keep him fixed in the corner of my eye, pretending not to notice, but I can't shake a feeling about him. He's like the current of the drainage ditches narrowly channelling their brown water into the Rio Grande. Every year a child drowns at the junction where whose currents meet, water such an unfamiliar element. It seems true that a person must be raised with something in order to assess all its dangers; unless you know how to read it the surface masks the drag and pull, the ways it can hurt.

The two men continue their talk, oblivious to my tequila demonstration, now discussing a politician called Le Pen and France being for *les vrais français,* the real French. Even among them there is this incessant categorization, this onion-like peeling of each other's skin. I am no less curious than when I would sneak into the bedroom before cartoons on Saturday, when I was no more than six, to watch the way Nick and my mother slept. I would breathe through my mouth and observe the way Mom's arm rested on his back in a mood of casual affection, the sort I rarely witnessed when they were awake. Nick's eyelids fluttered and I wondered if his dreams were reruns of that place he called Vietnam, where he toured twice because drugs were free. He worried at the sense of dampness he still felt, and how the persistent green of Asia swallowed sounds he could never take for granted, like footsteps and the rhythm of my mother sleeping next to him.

The bartender is serving another customer and I call to him.

—Nick, *une autre,* again, I say, pointing to my shot glass.

—*Je m'appelle Martin,* he says, annoyed.

Chapter twenty-two

The problem now is returning to the rue des Cannettes. It's as if I'm here and you're walking there, so drunk you can't make your fingers come into focus as your arm extends in front of you, arms and legs independent, multijointed, a marionette, and on these block-feet you must walk. You have no idea where everyone has gone, just gone, didn't even say goodbye but maybe they did and you just didn't hear them.

What time is it? No idea. *Aucune idée.* Probably the metro is closed already, but then, how could you be so dumb, you don't need to take the metro. Just walk home like you always do, but are you going to remember the way? Past the park and then a right and cut through the place Saint-Sulpice. How hard can it be.

—Martin, you shout, how much for the drinks? If he can't understand English, then too bad. But he says, *Attends,* wait, I'll check the tab.

This seems to happen very quickly: You're out the bar door and up the street before he turns back around. Figure, however much you owe is how much David, Michel, Martin, whatever, would have spent if he'd ever taken you on a real date. The universe finds order (did you say that out loud?). Then you're passing by the boucherie with its shining horse-head rimmed with a red band over the window; avoid looking at the meats left on display. *Cheval.*

Soon you slow down, momentum lost, and all you want to do is sleep, not even sleep really, just shut your eyes for a moment. You're walking boneless, pulling a mass with no structure. You have been smoking cigarettes and you breathe in and everywhere the taste of ash or its suggestion.

For all the spin and waves of nausea at least your thoughts have calmed, no hum, no white noise, only a clear kind of silence. You aren't sure where you are but it occurs to you that you need to be by the river, that the river leads in the direction you must go. Your mother used to say that where she grew up there was the Charles, the spine of Boston feeding into the Atlantic, and some bridge with four little towers she called "garrets". (What was the name of that bridge?) You asked, What color is so much water? And she said most days the Atlantic is a deep green, so green it looks gray, the Charles like a tarnished metal.

And now you're walking downhill, could be the rue de la Montagne Sainte-Geneviève, but then, you never truly know where you are because somehow one street always looks like the next. You become aware that the movement of the dress against your legs rasps like burlap, cumbersome, restrictive. You reach down with the intent of unbuttoning a few white buttons, but the holes are so small. So very, very small. The buttons pop off at the end and some in the middle and they spray out like buck-shot and you think, how can this be reassembled?

You get down on your knees to search for the buttons, it's your best dress and now what will you have, nothing. But this was a mistake, because you're not going to be able to get back up and you feel hot, think it must be a fever, influenza, when was it that women used to die left and right of consumption? But at least it can't be malaria, your mother protected you from that. You remember. She said, *The summer I was pregnant with you it was so hot I drank gin-and-tonics like they were going out of style. You'll never get malaria with all that quinine water in your system, baby.* Now beads of sweat well on the surface of your skin and are rolling down your face the way the tears roll down, scalding. You lean your heavy body into a doorway to rest, though you didn't realize there was a doorway until now, and you can't remember what you were just about to think. *je n'en peux plus,* you say to yourself. I can't go any farther, I can't do any more.

—*Comment? Qu'est-ce que dis, toi?* From above comes this high-pitched male voice asking you what it is you're saying. It addresses you in the familiar form but it's not a voice you recognize. But that's no surprise, there are millions of voices here, it's not some small town after all, but then, where are you, exactly? Maybe you are in fact back home and have only been dreaming of men with strange hands and one with black hair and so many women who never smile at each other and a language that pulls itself tighter around your throat like a snake, like a noose.

Look up and there is nothing but the broad, green neon cross, signifying a pharmacy, explaining what kind of a doorway you're in. The shadow of someone. You hold your arms up as if to be lifted, but the shadow pushes you back roughly, mumbles something or maybe you're just not hearing, but you do catch the word, *pute,* whore. Under the lime-colored light of the pharmacy flashes a brown, dead tooth, perhaps a grin, and then you're being pulled and kneaded, a bruising pressure, your dress torn farther open, a remaining button arcs through the air.

Other raw moments. The screaming of your mother and grandmother, how they went at each other like coyotes catching the scent of blood in the night. Your grandmother was saying, Is this any way to raise a kid? Why do you want to live like a goddamn Mexican? Your mother's needle-toed boots sunk into her shin in reply, and then Grand on the carpet, platinum strands from your mother's head streaming out of her clenched fist like the silk of corn stalks. You were, how old? In the middle, where you had been before, pushing them apart, but this time instinct and drive-through liquor had taken both of them over.

A stray fist cracked into the side of your head. It only hurt afterward, but it sobered them. They stopped to come pick you up, sobbing, saying, See what you did, each to the other.

How you had shaken off their hands as if shedding skin (in shock you would have said later, had you ever told anyone). You never thought you could be hurt, and you said in a smooth, calibrated voice that sounded so old coming from your mouth, just leave me alone. And there was a long sprint out to the pasture to look for a ride out, grabbing a halter and lead rope from the barn (that same barn). Screeching from the two of them behind you, their calls to come back.

The instant seemed as if it had already been snapped by a camera and I was just observing the photo in better light. Now life breaks into real time and no longer am I boneless. A power arrives that must be wholly my own, though I cannot say where it resides.

—*Lâche-moi! Espèce de con! Enculé, sale enculé!* Let go of me you dirty rotten motherfucker! My knee jams straight into his crotch, as he's unbalanced I twist my arm free and then begin to pound. My body takes over, it knows what to do, just feel the connection of my feet and my fists and the broad slap of my open palm over flesh, until somehow our places become reversed. I vaguely note how much smaller he is than I am, how shrivelled.

But there is no time for any sort of consideration because he has not felt enough yet, this isn't even close to being extinguished. How my back torques and my arm keeps straight, connecting again and again to his face and his chest, kicking his legs, trying to snap them like twigs. There is no way to calculate the force of what is raining down upon him, what he is repeating. I rip at his shirt pocket, certain I'll find my own hair coiled there.

—What were you thinking, moron? Who did you think I was? My body jerks as each breath catches.

What. The. Fuck.

Chapter twenty-three

An accident of geography that Praquin's studio should be the quickest location that will take me off the street. He does not turn on a lamp but the obscure light of moon through the window is bright enough for me to see that he's lying propped by pillows on the futon bed, the stubby ember of his Gauloise and the thick, acerbic smoke like fumigation. Graying chest-hairs sprout over the neckline of his cotton T-shirt. I apologize for waking him but he only shrugs, taps the end of his cigarette against an aluminum ashtray, smudged and blackened by use.

—*Qu'est-ce qui t'est arrivé?* What happened to you? he asks with mild curiosity, although he makes no effort to bridle his annoyance. He doesn't wait for a reply before he tells me that a girl should not walk around the streets at this hour.

—I walk around the streets at any hour.

He says that is a ridiculous thing to do. *Ne sois pas con.* Don't be so stupid.

—I don't have money for taxis.

—Of course you don't have money for taxis. He does not talk

so much as bite words. Let's not make this complicated. Just sleep here.

—*Je ne veux pas vous deranger,* I don't want to bother you, I protest, regretting the drunken impulse to seek shelter, knowing I have trampled certain lines of etiquette, so much more ephemeral than mere grammar, reminding me that words are not the difficult part; it's everything that falls between them.

—*Tu crois que tout est simple comme bonjour?* You think everything is as easy as that? In a voice meant to pierce he snaps, Well you've already bothered me, so just shut up and sleep here. Only a few more hours are left of the night.

Reduced, feeling worn to a nub, I lie on top of the covers, bothering only to remove my shoes. There is dirt in my scalp. I grate at it with fingernails broken and sharp.

Reflections from the street move over the ceiling like shadows made iridescent. I turn my head to look at the canvases and figures in various stages of development, the sweeps of color I cannot decipher in the light, the grace of a rounded edge. Their beauty, in all their various forms, strikes me and tears begin to sting my eyes. Why is it that such a man, whose face is an aftermath, who does not shut his mouth when he chews, can know creation and acts of invention, never questioning his right to them?

The bed jiggles and then his coarse hand reaches in the dark and leads to his crotch, the thing already bent upward and full.

—*Au moins tu peux me parler americain,* he says. At least you can speak American to me.

It's as if a switch has been pulled and your whole body shuts down, but somewhere a light is left on, enough to reason with, enough to understand that this perhaps is something you deserve, another situation you have brought upon yourself. His skin is warm in the way of a sleeping animal. Your natural body temperature is cold, a product of bad circulation, likely a portent of heart attack later in life. It has always bothered you to be so cool, but now you understand it is an evolutionary detail, a kind of calcification, like thistle or horns.

The graying of dawn. I rise too quickly from the futon and my dress crumples to my feet.

—*Tiens,* Praquin exclaims, *ça ne va pas,* this won't do. Only now does he observe the scrapes on my skin. Bruises blossom as purple-green flowers on my thighs, elbows grated and cracking. My ribs stick out like I've swallowed a cage but the curve of abdomen extends, potbellied, and my jaw is swollen.

I am about to reassure him that I am not really hurt, I made it through okay, just a few surface wounds. But he reaches over and pinches a fold of skin over my hip. Turns away. He sits up on the corner of the bed, puts a hand to his forehead and rubs.

—*Génial,* he says. *Quelle espèce de tartignolle tu es.* What a mess you are.

I stand in the middle of this cold floor with nothing between me and the morning air but the spark of some remote feeling, keeping me warm.

—You should have seen the other guy, I tell him, and don't bother with translation. What has lead me to this? Can $400 explain this? Why was this man, no actual meat to his lips, just skin tucked around a hole, left in charge of passing all judgement? And who told the French they were endowed with the vision to see clearly that which is wrong with the rest of the world?

At once I am overcome by a sense of loss so strong it nearly buckles my knees. All the days and hours I used to absorb this language, so unbearably distant, embraced it like a religion, the path to a salvation I could not picture but knew must exist. The way I have struggled to bring it into me, but it won't come closer. This frustration so deep it snaps my head back. The sharp intake of breath.

I walk to where he still cradles his forehead and touch his bristled cheek with the back of one finger.

—*Je ne te plais pas?* You don't like me like this? I say softly as I move my fingers further back through the anaemic strands of hair on the back of his head, feel the roll of flesh form as he lifts his eye to me. The look says he doesn't see the next move coming.

—*Tant pis, cochon.* Too damn bad. I bite off each syllable, shove his head sideways, unbalancing him from the bed and he topples to the floor, landing dog-like on all fours.

—Pay me what you owe me and then I'm out of here. *Je m'en vais. Vous comprenez?*

I move to grab the remnants of my dress and he still crouches on the floor where he landed. He's quiet, but as I look closer I see his belly move, his shoulders shake. It crosses my mind he may be experiencing some kind of seizure, but then I realize it's the first time I have seen him laugh.

—*Tu craques. Je me demandais quand ça arriverait.* I was wondering how long it would take you to lose it. He extends a hand to say, Help me up.

I do, for lack of another idea. He pats my back with his thick hand and tells me, Well done, *ma belle.* Let us resume work tomorrow.

Friday

Chapter twenty-four

Pascale wants me to get out of the bathroom. The staccato rap at the door and although her fist is only big enough to hold a hummingbird she's using all her knuckles. *Sabine, s'il te plaît.*

I fold myself down into the small tub so my knees come up as my head submerges but even underwater the vibrations of the knocks still reach my ears. I tilt my face so my mouth and nose break the surface of the water and think, Goddamn it. *Laisse-moi tranquille,* leave me alone.

—*Pascale? Pardon, je ne savais pas que to étais là,* I didn't even know you were there, I tell her at a low volume, the odd ripple as my lips move water. This is the code for why did you leave me in the bar, but of course to say that directly would not be *vache,* not quick enough, not sharp enough. In French to be forthright when you have your feelings hurt implies you are desperate, and, worse, stupid.

I reach a hand across my midriff and although no one would notice it I do, the hardness there, the knot, and I press my thumb deep into it until the broken edge of my nail cuts the skin. Blood dilutes quickly and becomes translucent as water. Just dig it out, dig it out and be done with it.

Even through the door, through the water, I can hear as Pascale sucks her lower lip and makes a clucking sound.

—*Dépêche-toi,* Hurry up, she says. *Je dois faire pipi.*

I push myself up from the tub and step onto the patch of towel, water dripping down to the tiles, my skin still pink. *Okay, je sors,* I'm coming.

As I reach to the back of the door for my robe, a man's oversized cotton shirt (Mom said, Nick won't need this anymore), the latch turns and Pascale's hand darts through.

Why do I feel frantic and quickly slam the door, nearly catching her thin wrist to be fractured like blown glass, why do I all at once gulp and then feel shaky, move to sit on the edge of the tub? Shame is the feeling of never being able to hide anything.

—*Je sors.* I'm getting out, please wait. I'm pleading, meek as a sheep. Why? *Attends. Je sors.*

Seconds later I emerge from the bathroom still wet and boiled-looking. Pascale scuttles past, no eye contact. What is there to say because what there is to begin cannot be easily ended, and this bright morning is no time for such talk. Slip my jeans on and a turtleneck and walk over to the kitchen sink where at least I know there's something to do.

There is the roaring flush, and then a blank moment, and then I start to arrange the small pan on the stove. Her small voice breaks through the clank of moving utensils.

—Bean, please to make the eggs scrambled, she says, holding three brownshelled eggs in her hands, extending them, but it is not this that signals her effort to *se réconcilier,* make up. The olive-branch is the words she puts forward in English, which she has never spoken to me before. She is saying she enjoyed learning songs, that perhaps she misjudged and assumed I was otherwise occupied at the bar.

Tears well in my eyes and I quickly shake them away as I would a fly or any other annoyance. I take the eggs.

—Scrambled, coming up.

Chapter twenty-five

This afternoon hangs so low, so gray, the clouds are in my hair. I have taken my day's money allowance for food and used it to buy a cheap ticket at the theater on the place de l'Odéon, on the boulevard Saint-Germain, the movie theater full except for the back rows. More than food I need this darkness, like time suspended, nothing grows or falls in these encapsulated moments. For two hours the only existence will be lives on a screen.

This is a French movie in the tradition of Truffaut but not as accomplished. The main character will sleep with her husband's best friend and either she will die or the three will go for coffee and that will end the film. I remember having to watch these movies in Miss Ortiz's class and how tense they made me, never going anywhere, no solution or balm, a series of knots no one cared enough to untie. Now they offer a measure of reassurance; I understand that French life is exactly French cinema. They just transfer it to celluloid, as few edits as possible.

The game I play by myself like solitaire is to invent new dialogue, give the characters real reasons to be unhappy. The goal is to do this all in French, but often I fall behind so I cheat and use English, Spanish, whatever keeps the stream flowing. The words melt together, the three whipping into one, and suddenly I'm speaking a new language, quietly, under my breath. My body folded up, arms hugging knees I tuck up to my chin, my feet on the back of the seat in front of me. Often I remember to pull my shoulders back and down, keep my back rigid, but this is not one of those times and my body collapses on itself, chest shallow and arms folded.

There's a rustle along my row, someone coughs and then a whisper asking if the seat near me is taken. I shake my head, irritated at the interruption. Just that one second and already I'm so far behind the dialogue in the scene I'll never catch up. I hate being behind the beat of anything, this ingrained pattern of knowing which way to turn, anticipate sudden change.

—She gets run over, says a man so close his breath brushes my ear. I saw this yesterday.

Unexpected. Peels me out of my skin. His voice deep and confiding.

I glance sideways in my thin-backed seat to see a man next to me with his head resting on his hands.

—Thanks for trying to ruin the end for me, but I already figured that out, I reply, my eyes back on the screen. I'm sorry, but do I know you?

—How'd you figure it out? The end, I mean?

—Everything ends badly.

—That's a very young thing for you to say, he says, and there might be a laugh in his voice.

—*Monsieur, du silence,* I begin, indignant, then it occurs to me we have been speaking English. What the hell? I say, turning to look at him more closely. Spindles of damp hair like someone come in from the rain obscure his features, but even in the dark theater the whites of his eyes shine. Light from the screen flickers weak but enough to see the frayed edges of his shirt cuff, the small pills of wool at the elbow corner of his sweater. It can't be.

—Did I meet you the other day? McDonalds?

He nods. I'm Abe, he says, extending a hand.

I ignore it. Is this just a weird coincidence or did you follow me here?

He draws his hand back. Coincidence.

Of course.

We sit withdrawn. I understand what it feels like to have been mauled, and so forever approach any dog with caution.

—Can I ask you if you're clinically paranoid or just moody?

—I bet you say that to all the girls.

On screen the character is walking down the street, and now there's a cut-away shot to a car careening towards her.

—I knew she was going to get it from the beginning, I say out loud, more to myself than to him.

He puts a finger over his lips to say, Quiet, and points to the screen.

—Quiet? Quiet? I turn to face him, not bothering to lower my voice. It feels good to speak English, but it surprises me when my words lurch forward like a bad clutch. Who... what do you think you are? Telling me what to do?

From the very back row come disgruntled murmurs and someone spits out, *Ta gueule, merde!* Shut the hell up! Abe shrugs, as if to say, see?

—I was just trying to tell you there's a good scene coming up.

—A good scene, are you kidding? This rates right up there with a home movie.

—It's about to end, he says, nonplussed.

—I don't care about the end.

He leans closer in. You will, he whispers, the coarse waves of his hair graze my cheek as his mouth comes close to my ear.

—Why are you whispering in my ear?

—Reverence for the dark.

In the movie the car is now barrelling toward the woman as she stands, resigned to the moment of impact. Then, from out of nowhere an arm jerks her to the sidewalk just as the car screams past.

The saviour is the husband she left a few dozen scenes earlier. They stand, both shaking and crying, clenched in embrace as the camera pans out to a city shot. I turn to him.

—But you said she got run over.

—I lied, he says unabashed. Disappointed?

—That you lied?

—That you were wrong about the tragic end, he says.

He makes me feel unlaced. As a form of apology I now offer my hand. I'm Sabine.

—Very pleased to know you, he says, the enamel of his smile revealed.

And I don't anticipate this, the feeling that comes with touching his hand. That shot of blue, the conduction there. There is a sense of being pulled in a warm tide. I imagine his lips suddenly on mine, the dime-store-candy scent of his breath. My hands could reach to touch the grating skin of his neck, one finger would draw a line down the column of his throat and I'm the one whose hungry. He would be the one to finally push away.

But instead we sit side by side, the edge of our hands not quite touching on the arm rest. I breathe shallow as if any sudden movement would trip the wires. The credits are rolling.

—Abe?

—Just watch, he says, there's a final shot of them kissing. It's almost Hollywood.

—Abe, I tell him, I'm not French.

—I know, he says, his eyes still on the screen. I'm not American.

Chapter twenty-six

It is this way after the cinema, my eyes and his blinded by the average light of the early afternoon, like moles, bumping into the glass of the door as the two of us push out onto the sidewalk at the place de l'Odéon. Everything blurred at the edges, too white, over exposed. The noise of passing traffic amplified along the wide boulevard. While my hearing is still open I am aware of the ambient sounds of the city breathing. On the sidewalk a shrivelled horn player in wrinkled brown layers sits to my left on the concrete, playing for centimes. Thin brass coins line the worn velvet of his instrument case, haphazard sequins. Abe reaches into his pocket and throws down a blue-colored bill.

—*Merci de votre générosité,* the old musician says, eyeing the fifty-franc note.

—*C'est avec plaisir,* he responds genuinely, the greater gift of respect in his voice. The weight of my arrogance falls upon me, how I assumed he fell neatly into a category and I shudder at this, guilty of the crime so often committed against me. I think of how sure I was of my appeal in the theater's surround black with only the chrome light off the screen to distort the curve of my face. Now in the sunlight when the icing melts you know what you are: knob knees, weak chin, thick waist, not what anyone expected at first glance.

We stand together, not talking. He looks this way and that, up and down the street, as if searching for a taxi or expecting a ride. The light also hits him, revealing the details I failed to take in before, traces of acne scars along his temple, the premature lines that have begun to form across his brow, suggesting a person who has had to take life seriously, concentration, worry and fatigue honing his face, giving him angles.

I am anticipating a quick goodbye, perhaps a brief noting what coincidence can bring, and then we will both walk away. This is just one of those things, a chance interaction, there are no recriminations, we meet and then we go, his name written nowhere. At any rate there is the situation with Praquin to handle. So I turn, thinking I'll walk down the street toward the iron-speared fence of the crumbling ruins of Cluny abbey, its mud color so like the desert adobe, like that one biting curve of country road and how often I would gun the rattling truck engine over that curve, the spin of tires on loose dirt, mocking the possibilities for disappearance on the *Jornada del Meurto*.

—Sabine? Abe calls, the brief touch of his hand on my arm makes me jump and pull away, a reflex, much like that point when sleep finally comes, dreaming of falling off a cliff, body jerking at the moment of impact.

—Do you have to be anywhere? I was going to have lunch. Maybe you'll join me this time?

I sense uncertainty in his tone and it pleases me. He does not expect or assume, he looks me square in the eye. Something within me shifts, it is a question of degree but still significant. I picture Praquin's scowl, the hot flow of words when it is ten, then fifteen then twenty minutes past the hour and still I do not show.

—Only if you'll tell me why you let me think you were American, I say.

—Because you wanted me to be, he says, stepping backward off the curb. We're going to have to cross the street, he says, unconsciously running his hand down the inside of my arm to grasp my hand, pulling me onto the street to braid through traffic, horns bleating as we pass. But I am thinking of the polite pressure of his fingers, as if leading a child at a busy crossing.

The Mouton Enragé is not one of the restaurants that ever makes it into the guide books, no wider than a boxcar, room for only four tables, the furniture neat but worn and irregular, and at the corners bubbles appear in the wallpaper. In a year it will sag. Still, it is possible to eat for under ten francs and retain some dignity. The waiter (his shaved eyebrows and talon fingernails suggest other employment) greets everyone with a heartfelt *bonjour,* there will be the runny foam topping each espresso, a lemon peel curving its razed yellow edge into the china cup. I think of Styrofoam cups from the 7-Eleven, microwaved burritos still in their plastic sheathes, and I believe that with so much grace for living the French should be much happier.

We sit stiffly like two pilgrims, unsure of what to say now that the logistics of arriving at the restaurant are resolved. He eyes the menu, wants to know what I'm having.

—Croque-monsieur. Best to play it safe.

—I'd go for the couscous if I were you, he says. The waiter's Berber. I'd take that as a sign.

I eat here at least once a week and I have never noticed the waiter looks like anything but a woman. I ask, How can you tell?

He leans a bit more forward across the table, mocks in an exaggerated secret-agent kind of whisper, We Arabs have ways of spotting our own.

I don't know why this should take me aback but it does. The comments everywhere about the Arabs are like background noise to me, nothing I could paint in detail but always there, the French phobia about their culture passing to brown hands, their cathedrals falling by attrition to a mongrel horde. And here the face of it all of it sits in front of me, handsome, intense. I want to laugh.

—I would have guessed Hispanic, I say lamely, knowing I've let the moment stretch too long before reply.

He considers this.

—Technically, I suppose I am. The Moors, you know? They got around. He absently motions as if to touch the hair fallen around my shoulders. I sit straighter to avoid the contact.

—I would have guessed you were Algerian, he says, *pied noir* maybe.

—And now? What kind of American am I?

—Someplace out West, right? Not California. Maybe Arizona? Colorado?

—Close enough.

I see her tiny porcelain figurines lined against the bay window shelves in the living-room, vainly trying to hold back the gray expanse of the desert in winter. She could not stop it because we were already a part of it, the buffalo grass and ocotillo, twisting its thorny spines upward, like reaching for air. The force of the desert shapes everything, and us, softer than sandstone.

*   *   *

His name is Ibrihim Afra, but in San Diego the other kids just called him Abe. His parents sent him there to live with an uncle in 1975 when Beirut exploded, Muslim against Christian. He was twelve, a soft down appeared on his upper lip. His mother knew someone would give him a gun. She made it out to France with his sister.

—And your father?

—They called Beirut the Paris of the Middle East, did you know that? he says, staring down into his plate, the cold grains of couscous like birdseed here and there.

—But what about your father?

—Let's talk about something else.

Chapter twenty-seven

We sit next to each other on the steps of Montmartre with tourists who are wearing shorts, as if by sheer will they can create a summer holiday. If it were not overcast the view from this hill would show the city laid out in delicate hues, past the train station to the Seine and the many green boughs of the Bois de Boulogne. To the far left there would stand the surreal white arch of La Defense and the metallic spokes of the skyscrapers there, the new center of industry.

—I always forget what Paris is like, he says, so whenever I'm here it surprises me all over again.

I wonder if I will ever say that, if I will forget the exact nature of the oxide tincture streaked down old metal roofs and the verdigris pattern that creates, the conga pulse from the African buskers in the metro. I wonder when I will stop talking to myself in French, each sentence a melody, erasing all before them so there is only this instant and one word following the next. *Encore le matin gris.*

Will I forget the steam rising off the baguettes, gliding over my face, how the very scent of it nourishes, the snap and crumble of crust? And years from now, wherever I am, will I remember the challenge of shopping for groceries at the UniPrix, much like Safeway except there's an escalator down. The cheese section smells like goats in a pen, the hint of mold and other things growing, but there is also the section *du vêtement* where I always linger for a moment near the lingerie racks on the way to buy boxed milk, finger the edges of lace; although they're only polyester they still feel nice. The French so willing to put unfamiliar ideas next to each other.

—But you never see a blue sky in Paris. I mean the real kind of blue, he says, his chin cradled between his palms. The blue that hurts to look at.

It occurs to me that were I to have met him back home, if he had just happened through on the interstate, I would not have to explain things like Mesilla's autumn air, because he would smell it too, the floating spice of chile roasting outside the supermarkets and how capsaicin pinches the senses. All these months, as bad as I have felt among the French, I have felt even worse upon those chance meetings of other Americans, their clean, scrubbed faces, the security of the junior year abroad, their degrees to come from Yale or Brown and the way they say, now *where* are you from again? The sly checking of the other's French and that painful clatter.

—If I had to live here forever, he is saying, that's what I'd miss most.

—No, I tell him. You'd think of other things.

—Like what? he asks. It is difficult to look into his eyes, their heavy rims, the way the mink hue absorbs light. What does Sabine think of? He nudges me, bumping my shoulder as if to dislodge whatever there is to come out.

I shrug. People. Mostly she thinks of people.

I want to tell a story based on my family, one in Technicolor, no close-ups, but I cannot manage even the first sentence. What could Nick be called? A form of uncle, attached to the mother but not the child? And to say "he was" would not be true, because that would mean he no longer exists, which is to say there is no wind because it cannot be seen. And anyway, the story would go that it was the mother who was, for all intents and purposes, the one who left, deflated by, what? Grief? And what of Sabine now, who again on Monday (don't think how close that is) must finish what was wrongly begun. It can only be said that she thinks of the dead ones and the drunk ones and the ones who will never been seen.

It just seems right to put a hand on his arm. He does not grab it for more urgent or closer contact, nor does he push it away. He leaves it there, as if he can carry the burden of it. Tears brim over and run down, but they do not sting. They slide easily. There is no painful gasp to catch a breath. If I were to bury my face harder against his arm, the wool from his sweater would absorb the moisture, and the tears would be gone, as if they never had appeared.

Near dark, the Seine like a flow of liquid charcoal on which move the *bateaux-mouches,* their lights creating one long floating sapphire wave.

—I've never liked the water, I say.

—Afraid? Can't you swim?

I start to rebuff the suggestion, no, of course I'm not afraid, but the look in his eyes and the easy smile of his face mean he knows what it is to be afraid.

I tell him of La Llorona, the ghost woman by the river, the stories told to me as I was wrapped under covers (cardboard never stopped the draft from the broken window in the hall), Nick with his lips smelling good like masa, saying, Never go down by the river, *hija.* La Llorona will get you. I would pretend not to be afraid when he said she waited at the Rio Grande to drag children into the water and hold them in the undertow. I could see that her back would be deformed and bent from these centuries of walking, the bellow of her sadness as she pulled dried grass from the banks, putting the withering stalks on her head in need of hair. Later I would deny the logic of the story, telling Nick, No old crone with chalk bones could hold me. He would say, See, you're all full of pride. That's how she gets you.

Nick would recite the story of La Llorona even when I was

old enough to know about legends and myths, when the silver tabby named Chloe who lived in the barn got run over by Robbie Taffoya's four-wheel drive. The kittens she left were not more than a day old. He put them gently in a burlap bag, prying my hands from them, saying, Their mother can't care for them, *bija* and they're too young to make it on their own. He said, I'm giving them to La Llorona. It's all she wants, babies of her own.

—Yes, I tell him finally. Yes, I'm afraid.

He reaches into the collar of his sweater and pulls out a thin silver chain, slips it from around his neck.

—Here, he says, take this. It's stronger than La Llorona. He lays the chain in my palm, a round, silver medal attached. I turn it in my hand to examine the milky turquoise enamel face, the image of a man carrying a child across his back, St Christopher with baby Jesus and the weight of the world strapped to his back.

—My mother had it blessed by a bishop, he says. She's into that kind of thing.

—I couldn't take this from you. Protesting, I try to hand it back.

—You're not taking it. I'm giving it, he says, wrapping his hand over mine. It can't hurt.

We stay like that, fist over fist, silent for a moment. It starts to rain.

—Come on, he says, standing, not letting go of my hand. My apartment is on this side of the river.

I look up at him.

—What's that supposed to mean?

—It means let's get out of the rain.

Chapter twenty-eight

Rain like gravel strikes the window-pane, cold hangs in the corners. His worn clothes gave no hint of what this apartment near the Opéra would be, the old, high ceilings, the gold Louis Quatorze trim, the thick carpet smooth and blue, suggesting the Mediterranean could be walked across. Narrow halls, many closed doors. So far from the boulevard it doesn't need curtains across the wide arches of window. The careful interior surprises me: a gilded mirror, a painting of a countryside view, the minute fissures in the oils indicating that it's not a print. I have never been in a home of such conscious harmony.

The rain drops running down the glass form a network of tributaries. *Il pleure dans mon coeur / Comme il pleut sur la ville / Quelle est cette langueur / Qui pénètre mon coeur?* I don't remember the end of that poem but those four lines of tears, rain and longing are a kind of mantra, the first that come to me when I hear the sound of rain or feel it on my skin. I do not know at what moment this happened but French has become the language of my head. I wonder if Miss Ortiz knew she was giving me the seeds that would offer the comfort of analysis and dissection, so that even decades from this moment I will be poised to explain an idea in English yet find myself stuck, unable to translate that which I have known only in French.

—On a good day you can see the white of Sacre Coeur, Abe says, coming to stand behind me. Although he does not touch I can feel the heat of his body wrapping around me, and how I want to sink back into that warmth, but I feel wrung out, worn, less than what I should be. This is bad timing, to meet someone just now who seems himself to need nothing but to move through the city hand in hand and share the ordinary. I cannot trust myself to judge, it is impossible to know if he would understand all the shades of gray I have learned to negotiate. I imagine the disgust that would cross his face if he knew all that I contain and the low places I know and, after everything, that disgust would be the last thing I could stand to see.

He puts a hand on my shoulder blade, reaches to touch my face and says, Look at me.

His lips are full and they touch me like summer.

—Don't, I say, shifting away, breaking his touch. I'm sorry, but I can't.

—Can't what? I'm not asking for anything.

—You will.

—You've got everything figured out already, uh? I hate to tell you this, but you don't know shit.

He moves two steps to the edge of a plush couch facing the window, in one fluid move pulls off his musty sweater still damp from the downpour, throws it to the carpet. He stretches back, taps a hand at the corner of his shoulder in a motion that means lay your head here. And of all the things I have done, this seems the most dangerous, to go to the couch and sit back, rest against the crook of shoulder. I put my palm across his heart to feel the rhythm there. He rests his chin on the top of my head.

—At sunrise, he says, the Sacre Coeur turns coral.

For the moment the rain has subsided. Abe stretches his legs, says there's nothing in the kitchen to drink.

—Stay here while I go get something? He has the habit of ending his sentences up like that, as though waiting for the world to give him answers.

When he stands I feel the rush of cold replace the warmth created where our bodies touched.

—Don't even think about moving, he says, backing away toward the door. I'll be back so fast you won't even know I'm gone.

—What are you still doing here then? Get! I say, a mock scolding tone.

When I hear the door close I jump up, intent on finding the toilet. Stumbling in the hallway, opening wrong doors, I finally find the bathroom, its tiny porcelain tiles, the tub with animal feet underneath. And two toothbrushes, one chewed and frayed, the other pristine. The further evidence isn't obvious, I have to look around for it, but sure enough there's the China blue eyeliner in the drawer next to the sink. This explains the blue carpet, the lingering powder scent, the thriving fern with its broad arms over the gilded plant-stand. And this sensation that I can't shake, like the current of another woman's breath at my neck. Why should it be otherwise?

I hold the liner in my hand, wondering, looking at the reflection staring back at me in the lead glass of the mirror over the top. It cannot be called chic, this reflection, just bare faced and unmanicured. There is nothing else to do but put the soft tip of the liner to the base of my lashes and pull. But it is too dark. Her eyes are a truer blue.

Chapter twenty-nine

When I return to the main room he is indeed back, opening a bottle of Beaujolais.

—*Comment elle s'appelle, ta fiancée?* By the way, what's your girlfriend's name? I say, tone practised and bored, the way my mother would say, Listen cowboy, this isn't my first barbecue. In French my voice is more distant, a step away, above petty schoolgirl feelings and the way disappointment can singe.

He comes in with glasses each half filled with the wine, hands one to me. He looks into my face, his eyes narrowing.

—The last girlfriend I had was named Isabelle. She left me for a Dutch anthropologist, so you can't mean *her,* he says, pressing closer to me so I have to lean back slightly to keep looking him in the eye. He says, Just a guess, but could you be talking about my mother?

He goes into another room, returns with a silver-framed picture, says, This woman? Is this who you mean?

In the photo his arm is around a woman with hair a gold too shiny to be real, like tinsel, her petite frame dressed in a pale pink suit that looks like something out of a magazine, adorned with a label like

Chanel, perhaps, or Dior. She is looking at her son, her cerulean eyes radiant, as if to say, See the glory I have produced in this world.

I hand the photo back, feeling doltish and small.

—You don't look like her, I say. I don't look like my mother, either.

He traces the face in the frame lightly. No dust has been allowed to collect. She's a German Turk, educated in Paris, he says, but my father used to call her Miss America.

He says this in a way that makes me know he wakes bound by sheets holding him down into dreams that scald, he knows what it is to search although you're not even certain of what is lost. I reach to him, my fingers quickly laced into that hair, the color of night.

He remembers it was the twenty-seventh night of Ramadan. In Arabic it is *Laylat el-Kdar,* the Night of Fate when the entire course of a person's life will be charted. He says it is described in the Koran as "the incomparable and marvellous night, the favored one among thousands of nights", although he does not read this book or any like it anymore.

His father was Muslim by birth, married to this Christian Turk, but it could be said he was first a businessman, too cosmopolitan for religion, a man who savoured Debussy and Degas. He said it was as if overnight the streets of Beirut were ripped apart like precious fabric, Palestinian and leftist militias against the Christian Phalange, others too numerous to name. His father did not fit neatly into any one category; they considered him a blight easily cleared when he walked down the street at dusk toward home, holding his son's hand. The bullets entered small but their exits created cavernous holes of gore.

—Did you check his pulse?

—Yes.

—Did you try to stem the blood with your own clothes, then finally with your hands, but it wouldn't stop coming?

—Yes.

—Did it seem that he was in pain too vast to measure? Was

his skin quickly cold? Did you pray to God that you could do something, anything?

—Of course.

—Did it surprise you that you didn't cry?

—How did you know?

His arms around me, we lay exhausted, like people escaped. There is an airless feeling, pressure wrapped around with the hum of high voltage wires.

—That season before I left the chile vines were covered in a red that seemed to bleed, I tell him, letting the tip of my index finger run along the ridge where his hip meets his abdominal muscles, the curve of his flesh firm and strong. He moans slightly between his closed lips, pulls me tighter.

—What does the Koran say about that, vines that bleed?

—It says that the Lord created man out of curdled blood. Maybe you were seeing the beginning of something, he says. He runs his hands up my arm, encircling the wrist between his index finger and thumb, stroking the blue vein that runs like a highway into my palm, burying his face in my hair, his breath sweet, like mint.

Chapter thirty

Abe sleeps. Hands open, palms bare. The lines, their finely sutured detail, run long, right into the rings where the skin of his wrist has folded again and again. To be able to read what is written there, imagine him living in the Lebanese summers layered under the hot breezes and grating winds, always waiting for the lean shadows of winter, the season that never really comes.

I have already memorized his expressions, the curve of brow, the crease of his smile and the way when irritation settles in his jaw, the muscles contract. He pinches the underside of his lip between his teeth when he's concentrating, heavy lids of his eyes when he touches my hand. But now his face is naked, lips slack, slightly parted. It is disquieting to see him without the controlled demeanour he has learned to offer the world, to see how much he trusts. The arch of his foot lies against my calf, his arm resting across my waist, close enough to accidentally graze the hardness there, so I move, but there is no place in this single-sized bed that doesn't contain at least an inch of him.

It will be easy to leave while he sleeps, no having to say where I'm going or why at this time of night. Easing up to sit on the edge of the bed, my feet land on the spines of paperbacks spread face down on the floor, covers curled at the edges. *Italian for Travelers* beneath my toes, three paper place-mats from McDonalds, one from Burger King, all imprinted with the Paris metro plan, are grouped like a small rug in front of the chair by the door, over which a huge backpack hangs on its Aluminum frame. Everything I see seems to facilitate movement, this room only a resting place.

I reach over to get my shoes and the bed-springs groan. He stirs. His eyes open but his face stays pressed against the pillow exactly as it did in sleep. He stretches an arm up and blankets the color of buttermilk fall away, exposing his chest.

—What are you doing getting up? he says.

—I can't sleep. I don't want to keep you awake.

—You can't be leaving.

—I am.

—It's raining too hard. You'll drown.

—Only if I look up at the sky. Besides, I say, tapping the medal hanging around my neck, I have protection.

He props himself up on an elbow, his hair on one side made pancake-even by the pillow, the other sticking straight out. He yawns. He is not bothered by self-consciousness. He reaches out and runs a hand over my hip bones.

—How did you get so bruised?

—I'm clumsy.

—The way you walk makes me think of low boats in a riptide, he says and he pounces, pulls me onto the bed, runs his hands up my sides, tickling. It hurts to laugh so hard.

After a moment he says, I hardly know anything about you. I want to know everything.

This extinguishes the laughter. There isn't much to tell, I say, flatly. I'm just the typical American girl.

—I won't let you up until you tell me something.

—You Arabs are always taking hostages.

—Exactly, he says, nipping my ear. Talk or I'll stone you like the heathen you are.

So this is what you do: tell him your mother went West when you were just an infant because she had to fall off the face of the known world, people always said she was trouble and a bastard kid just couldn't be tolerated. She never forgot a line from her high-school French text, *Je m'appelle Sabine,* and she would say, That's how you got your name. As a child you always wanted the French sentence repeated, you thought the sounds fell together the way music falls, escaping into air, perhaps understanding there was a current that led out.

She became a nurse and settled where there are supplies of soldiers always needing tending, a place with an interstate running through it and a needling sun. She would walk you to school in your kindergarten best along the irrigation ditches, a green velvet jumper and white patent leather shoes. She would clean the dust from the shoes with spit and a Kleenex from her purse before you walked into class. There was always a kiss goodbye, staining your cheek red or pink. Then she took up with Nick, who sometimes was an embracing, warm man, but who sometimes tied off and stored his blood in the refrigerator. If there was enough heroin in his system at the time he drew blood, the dope would be strong enough for a fix when he couldn't score, would get so junksick he couldn't walk. When those times came he'd drink it with a chaser of mescal and he'd say *Hija,* get me a beer, too.

And you, with your headphones, reciting French conversation tapes copied from school. The bedroom door of the trailer closed, but thin enough to dash with one good punch.

He holds me as if his arms can dam the flood before him.

—I'm so sorry, he says, kissing my temple. But you made it out. You're safe now.

If he knew how those words pierce, if he could see how I am

balanced on the brink, forward movement the only prospect. The weight of everything behind me makes it impossible not to teeter.

—Yes. I'm here, I tell him, grasping his hand. Go back to sleep. It's the middle of the night.

Saturday

Chapter thirty-one

I leave like a thief, not latching the door for fear its squeak will raise the sleeping. The morning could have brought complications, perhaps a strained silence, a sudden appointment remembered, promises to call. I can't risk that.

Very early morning. A fine mist lingers in the air like gauze, revealing sudden turns and steps before my eyes. I don't know my way around the Right Bank as well as the Left, and the metro is closed. I cross my arms across my chest and just keep walking, walking. Finally I come upon the industrial tubes of the Pompidou Center (how much like a hamster container) which signals I'm near Les Halles, where the ground seems lower, the mantle of earth trampled thin.

I find myself on a street not much wider than the span of my arms, the brick-lined path wet enough to look greased. There is no sound but the click of others' shoes, I notice dark forms passing, faces down. Women stand in portals one right next door to the next like no kind of sentries I've ever seen. The only light is filtered through curtains drawn in rooms high above, and I realize with a start that this is the special red of the rue Saint-Denis.

From nowhere she appears walking toward me, her dark mouth, diagonal-striped shirt stretched over her chest like new skin, her skirt a mere detail. She isn't tall but her body seems large, overripe, the way a peach looks in the days before it rots and falls to the ground. The winter air draws goosebumps on her exposed, black body, and her eyes are the shape of globes, shimmering violet applied thickly over each lid. She looks like the chaos from which worlds are born. I cannot take my eyes off her.

She notices my gaze, strides up to me so that no more than inches separate us. I mean to keep walking but I am transfixed.

—*Ne me regard pas comme ça.* Her voice defines wrath. Spittle collects in the corner of her mouth. Alcohol from twist-top bottles, pills that arrive in plastic bags, packets wrapped in tin foil, all produce this particular ugliness. *Vous et moi, nous sommes pareil,* we are exactly the same.

—*Pardon,* I murmur, eyes downcast. I move to get beyond her and suddenly she strikes wildly, backhanding me across the head. I huddle down, expecting I don't know what.

—*Vous n'avez pas le droit,* you don't have the right, she is screaming, walking past me, arms waving.

The tornado passes. I remain squatting in the street, the women in the doorways look past me as they would a stone. I feel a burning behind my eyes, a choking, my shoulders shake. All I ever seem to do now is cry.

What was left of the night is replaced with a blister-colored sunrise, the *bouqainists* begin to open their stalls along the Seine. The African street-cleaners sweep away dog shit made mud by the rain. Their faces are so solemn usually but one of the men smiles brightly at me; I reply with a small *bonjour.* I walk past a patisserie I have never noticed before, chocolate tops of the religieuses in the window, the smell like heaven come to earth. I have made it back to the sixth arrondissement.

Sunday

Chapter thirty-two

Madame Doumic is back from early morning mass, she eyes me up and down, greets me with a terse hello. I know I am rumpled, hair like wire, the evidence of the way I have been living written clearly. I have not been *prudente*. I do not care.

—*Un certain Monsieur Jean Praquin a téléphoné plusieurs fois hier,* Mr Praquin has called several times yesterday, she says, pulling several white notes out of the box and handing them to me.

—*Zut,* I say in a mock girlish way, pretending to read the messages. *Il est un vrai monstre sacré.* At last, a chance to use that long-ago conversation-tape phrase. I giggle to myself, it builds into a full-blown laugh. She does not find me amusing.

It is early but I am climbing the stairs to his studio, deciding what to say. Sorry, but I had something better to do. Sorry, I didn't want to do as I was told. Sorry, but what can you expect from a stupid American.

I give one hard rap on the door with the side of my fist as if to say, *Monsieur Praquin, êtes-vous là?* Are you there? I am staring at my one white blouse, realizing that I've missed a button again, the thing's all misaligned.

—*Qu'est-ce que to veux, toi?* What do you want? *Pourquoi tu m'emmerdes à cette heure?* Why are you bugging me at this hour? He opens the door with a look on his face like sour milk.

—*Desolée d'arriver sans prevenir, mais...* Midway through my apology for arriving without notice I look past the top of his head to see a young woman sitting on the futon, a terry robe tied at her waist, her hair long, not as curly as mine but close enough, and I realize that I'm looking at my replacement. He follows my gaze.

—*Bon ouei,* he says, the words for "well, yes," but which actually translate as no response at all and he shrugs, offers no more words.

Imagine feeling embarrassed the way prepubescent children feel embarrassed, as whenever a teacher made you stand at the chalk board, and you, with the knee-high naugahyde boots your mother bought at the TG&Y back-to-school sale, your hair orange, the summer spent trying for blonde with lemons and sun, broken like dry spaghetti, caught in rubber bands. I have sat in front of this man for hours, letting him take my body for his own forms but at this second I am more self-conscious than at any naked moment. I want to dry up and blow away.

But, fuck that.

Within there is a force strong enough to put me on a plane for this dreamed-of foreign place half the world away, the force that opened the big steel door the first day of class when my legs were wobbly with anticipation and my French was weak. The force that will do what has to be done.

I push past him and enter the cool room, go out of my way to say hello to the replacement. I turn to Praquin, who is yelling in that way the French do, without actually raising his voice, it sounds like he's swallowing marbles or breaking furniture with his mouth and I'm not paying any attention to the words.

—Just pay me, I tell him in English, holding my hand out flat.

He rushes toward me. *Va t'en!* Get the hell out of here!

It occurs to me that maybe he's not planning to give me money at all, maybe he never was or maybe he considers that missed session a forfeit, and all at once I don't feel so brave. Without that money there will be no *intervention,* no doctor's appointment, and that knot below my stomach will grow and bloat and the cycle will begin all over again, except that at least my mother has a trade, a skill with which to barter, and what have I but some half-remembered poems, a borrowed saint's medal, the hunger to absorb the world and know it.

My eyes lock on his face, red, I have never noticed how bloated.

—*Je partirai lorsque je serais payée,* I'll go with money in my hand. I say this calmly, in a polite tone, as if I were already saying thank you, goodbye.

He turns to the dresser and pulls out the tan and blue francs, odd that it has never occurred to me how much their colors are like fast-food wrappers. He holds them, drops them to scatter on the floor. He walks toward the window as if to walk through me. Me, already a vapour, already ceased to exist.

There cannot be more than 180 francs on the floor, but if I want any of them I will have to get down and pick them up.

Viewed from the course of a lifetime, this is the best of the worst things a person must do.

Knees bent, back bowed, fingers grab the worn francs.

Chapter thirty-three

It is possible to get all the way to Charles de Gaulle airport for free. It requires a series of connections, calculations regarding times, the number of passengers in any given train car, all of which factor into the probability of being asked to produce a ticket. The ability to jump the turnstile, or at least slip underneath, is vital, especially at the limit of the Périphérique where the metro turns into the rapid transit train, where the entrances are a more complicated series of reflective steel gates and spokes. Sometimes it is even necessary to wedge through two at a time with a stranger (preferably small in stature) who is kind enough to permit such a flagrant violation of the regulations.

The agent at the Air France desk is professionally cordial, she asks for identification, the *carte d'etudiant* will of course do. It is not a question of wanting to transfer the fare to another flight, so no credit voucher need be prepared. Just the refund for the amount of the return flight to El Paso, Texas via JFK with a six-hour layover in Dallas. The total should come to approximately $768.46. The dollar is strong against the franc but airport exchange rates are never as fair as those of the banks; nevertheless, they are immediately accessible, open weekends, twenty-four hours a day.

*   *   *

The ticket was zipped into the bottom compartment of my suitcase, tucked under the bed, exactly where I had placed it the first day I arrived (it may have been in April, just like the old song).

It is always a question of perspective, what at one degree or angle appears as inert matter will, when observed from another, entirely novel, unexplored vantage point, reveal itself as material exploding with potential. Although it may appear so, nothing is ever truly static but always on its way to becoming something else.

I have just erased the last vestige of the notion that the future should be charted with careful planning. I will now tell the truth as I know it: each moment is and has always been *terre inconnue.*

Monday

Chapter thirty-four

The phone is blaring at the crack of dawn, but I catch it on the second ring, Pascale still lightly snoring, me lying opened-eyed in bed, where I have lain curled like in a shell under the covers. I hold my appointment card in my hand. 9 AM It can't be the hospital on the other end of the line, no one is going to tell me now, Unfortunately, mademoiselle, we have reviewed the records and a miscalculation has been made. There is nothing that can be done now.

—*J'écoute*, I say, pinning the receiver between my shoulder and ear.

—*Bonjour* to you too, Abe says. The sound of his voice so unexpected, but he talks like he's known me all his life. As if he has always known the scars that pucker the folds at my knees, like he could tell the story about how, just entering fourth grade that year, I spun my bike out on the sharp gravel of the driveway.

I'm not big on pleasantries, I like to get straight to the point. I pull the blankets over my head, creating a little cave so Pascale won't hear me and complain. His voice creates surges much like uneven voltages of electricity, making every part of me feel charged, magnetized, weak in all connecting joints. I want to tell him I understand that attraction and the force of wind follow the same laws of physics, that they seem to be created from nothing and can be detected only by their power to move objects, pressing one to another. I want to tell him how good his voice sounds but all I end up with is, What are you doing up at this hour?

—Don't tell me you were finally getting some sleep and I woke you? He must be calling from a pay phone because his voice comes out in loud bursts, as if he's trying to hear it himself. His breath crackles over the line and it sounds as if he's cupping the receiver to siphon his voice into the phone.

—No. I swallow and shut my eyes but see images of him, the rise of muscle along his spine, the guttural break in his voice when you ask him, what is *this* in Arabic?

—I'm not going to ask why you left me *seul comme un chien*, alone like a dog, he begins. I've been thinking, and I've decided you were the little girl who had no heads on her dolls.

I wrap my fingers around the phone cord.

—Wrong. I just gave them haircuts.

For a moment there is nothing but the hollow echo of the receiver and finally he says, I'm at the Gare de Lyon, about to leave. It's the train for Milan.

I imagine his dark form there, underneath flickering green fluorescent tint, the white tiles along the wall looking gray.

—You can't be heading back to Beirut.

—Italy's only temporary, he says, I'll be there about a month. I'm trying to figure out what I want to do next. Take this phone number and address. The place is easy to find.

—What does that mean?

—It means I want to see my St Christopher medal, and you're going to have to come to Italy to show it to me, he says. Please, Sabine.

In the background perhaps I hear the hiss and grind of the train, perhaps I am just imagining the detail. I say, But I don't speak any Italian.

—We can make do, he says, his voice urgent. Hey, this is crazy, but why don't you come now, today?

—No, I say, too quick. I mean, I have an appointment. Vital.

—It can't be put off?

—Absolutely not. It's vital. Really.

—I understand, he says in a studied way that means I don't believe you. Listen, I've got to go.

—Abe? I say, wanting to hang on to the warm current of his voice. Please, give me the address in Italy. Please.

I scramble for a pen on the bedside table, write in small letters on the back of my appointment card.

—Good luck, he says.

—Abe? I say, but it is already too late, the dial tone flat, the line disconnected.

Chapter thirty-five

I am walking to the metro station just as I have always done but this morning I cannot breathe fast enough, my heart beats with an irregular rhythm, skin flushed and steaming even in the prickling chill of air (why do you always have the wrong thing on, Bean?). To the left stands the black-streaked bricks of the *église* Saint-Sulpice, how worn it looks, how plain. It has been said that there is no church more perfect than Notre Dame, with its finely drawn arches like webs, its first stone laid in 1163 by a pope, and if that is true then I think no church is more forlorn than Saint-Sulpice, which Madame Doumic explained was built as a parish for peasants: the asymmetrical details, the towers unfinished and irregular. They must have said, It's good enough for who it's for.

I have never once thought to go inside, but today, on the day when time has to be more carefully measured than all before it, I stop walking, turn to run up the steps, use both hands to pull the old door open.

The walls jut straight-angled and jagged, the color of hoofs, made waxy from tallow from candles burned before the Revolution or just a world war ago, no one left to remember which, and the smell of drying sweat and layers of clothes, even the faint implication of nicotine. Weak lights perched in the stone columns only blanch the skin and pattern shadows along the aisles, the oiled pews dark and gleaming.

Sit at the back because you know you don't have a right to sit closer to the altar, nearer the peering eyes of a priest or who knows, maybe even God, knowing what you've done, and what you are about to do, because it is in fact written indelibly on your skin. His voice would thunder, Get thee hence, Sinner, because didn't he say that in the Bible, or maybe that was Shakespeare, you can't remember where you read it.

   The wood is hard against your back and you feel the need to pray for something but you only half know the system for praying, there's a way to fold your hands and the words, Hail Mary Mother of God, but you don't remember if they come at the beginning or the end of the prayer, so you just bow your head and tuck your arms around your rib cage.

   When you're in church there should be an orderly method of arranging your thoughts, a sense of repentance, but you can't get your mind off Mary. Even though she knew her child's life would end in suffering she considered only the moments of light there would be, the difference one person can make. How does a woman become like Mary? When does she learn to measure the good so that it outweighs everything else? Then it hits you like a belt on raw flesh that, when everything else is stripped away, you are afraid for this conglomeration of cells that your body produces in spite of your denying it, that should it continue it would transform into a he or a she. But you cannot guarantee its safety, least of all in your hands, the hands of the mother, because you—let me say here "I"—I cannot trust myself not to do the things that have been done to me, the senseless, hard things that cannot be bandaged or balmed.

By the time I got to the porch, I could see my mother sitting on the stoop, the peroxide shine of her hair reflecting the full moonlight, bright as day.

—Mom, what's going on? I heard a gun. It was loud. I sit down beside her.

At first I didn't notice, thought only of how cold the wood felt against my bare leg and hoped I wouldn't get splinters from the old boards. Then I became conscious of a soft sucking sound and I looked at her face to see her lower lip pressed against her teeth in tiny rapid tugs. Tears ran into the crease of her nose and her unblinking eyes, how like colored glass they looked from the side.

—Mom, quit this. What's going on? I yelled this and stood up quickly, there was a trap-door feeling like the bottom had just been pulled out. What are you doing out here alone? Mom? I kept yelling as if volume would make a difference.

She looked up at me, as if at a piece of animation, in wonder that all the parts could move.

—All this time Bean, I thought he'd be okay, she said, her voice cracked and strange sounding, an uneven frequency, a vain transmission in the night.

I understood then. I put my hands on her shoulders, gently. Mom, where is he?

—The barn, she said, taking my hand to press it against her cheek, clenching her grip when I tried to pull away, and I became aware of her sticky fingers, the wet streaks down her robe appearing black in the light.

I would not scream, even though I wanted my words driven into her.

—Let's go see if he's Alright, I told her. Let's call the police.

—He's not Alright, she said, her voice suddenly strong. I checked. His head is just, shit, you know, his aim was bad. I can't believe he's still breathing, but I just couldn't, I don't want him to suffer, baby, you know? But I just couldn't.

A calm spread over my body, an overlay of denser material. My voice was careful, methodical. Are you sure? Positive? I said. It didn't just look like he was breathing?

She nodded, said, I found a pulse. Her grip slackened and I eased my hand away.

—You need to call the police, Mom, I said, kissing her forehead, helping her stand, watching as she moved into the trailer to the phone. Then I turned and closed the screen door quietly behind me as I stepped onto the gravel of the driveway. Nick's truck was parked there, the driver side door open, the rifle missing from the rack on the rear cab window. I leaned in, my fingers feeling for the lead points, their brass casings. I held two in my hand as I headed for the barn, steps even, sure of my aim.

I cannot cry and I cannot linger in here, because to do that would be to pull the last thread. What it comes down to is the fact that I cannot make it better for anyone else.

Chapter thirty-six

Standing in front of the Hôpital Saint-Louis, considering whether I should get a taxi or walk to the metro, not a half hour after the abortion. *L'avortement* was not the word today. *L'intervention,* the surgery, to intervene, to step in and thus alter the course, to hog-tie the hands of Fate and say to him, *I may be gutted and bleeding but this time, you bastard, I beat you.* Such things all wrapped so discretely in the word. *L'intervention.* Hand it to them, because if nothing else the French avoid the prosaic, all those things forever better left unsaid.

It is raining now but with no force and I think nothing here has a punch. There is a moment between raindrops hitting my face when I wonder what being pregnant would have been like and having a child who was French, at least half. Perhaps years from now a child will accidentally bump into me while playing in a park and I will look into its eyes and wonder at those I never saw. And I wonder if it would have been born knowing the price of everything and been used up and awful but otherwise full of loveliness like everyone I have known here.

A woman walks her dog and it stops to shit on the sidewalk in front of the hospital, which was built after the plagues as if its mere construction could act as a kind of talisman against contagion. She leaves the pile there in front of me and I think, how foul.

—*Dégueulasse,* I yell, but she doesn't turn her head.

I stand in the street wiped by the rain, wet and soggy, the air smelling of ancient bacteria, and I believe I can feel the winding down, the exact instant the self grows older. This city is a deception and I have known many things too soon, but that is nothing to be ashamed about. I came here not to lose but to find another self, the one who knows how to use the right spoon and fork, match the perfect shade of lipstick and have the gracious comment necessary for anything unexpected in life. But I don't have the dialogue memorized, even if the accent has been mastered.

And I never will. How good that feels to say.

Now I can begin to imagine the day when it will be as if these French words were never spoken, when I will not need to remember vocabulary because the structure of all language will remain as a frame, how it is conjured from the brain, a means but not an end.

These days will soon be over and I have no more answers than before and there will be so many questions. Yet, Paris has taught me the meaning of pastel and the light, this exact angle, how much like a touch it is across your face and the smell of cloves and things retained on the streets where feet have worn grooves in the sidewalk. Here I have known beauty, and it is messy and wet at its fleshy core. Still, the desire to be amidst it.

The only thing I recall from this morning is that part in my delirium after the black rubber mask spread across my face when the nurse said *Ne t'inquiet pas, ma petite,* Don't worry, sweetie and I panicked and grabbed her hand because somehow I had to explain exactly why this had to happen. I was so afraid she would assume this choice was the easiest one, so I had to be heard, I tried to say, no, listen, this is the hard part. I woke up in a room with other women, lined in rows of beds, stretched out like casualties. Some moaned.

My fingers clasped the medal I'd told Abe I would return and now I believe that, yes, nothing will keep me from that promise.

Now a taxi stops and the driver rolls down his window. He speaks French so badly I wonder if there is not another medium in which we can exchange information. He doesn't ask what I've been doing in this public hospital for the poor and foreign where moss laces brick like mortar (during *la Révolution* it doubled as a prison for nobles, who were guillotined near the square).

I start to tell him where I need to go and he looks confused, so I extend a small courtesy smile and wave him on. It is easier to walk. I know where I am going and it strikes me as a small miracle that I can know the layout so well when I have come from a place where blue cannot be contained by the sky, where doors are hollow.

As I follow the sidewalk along the street I notice for the first time the pocked edges of brick and the grainy, unremarkable shape of the objects that make up such a city and I marvel at how splendour can be created here, yet it is. I feel grateful to have walked this city, and I consider crossing the river at the Pont des Beaux Arts with my raw hips. Then I'd like to walk to the Ile Saint-Louis for ice cream but I can't remember the name of the shop and, besides, my body feels scoured and vacant. There is an ache unlike any I have ever felt and I sense there will be permanent scarring. Something is wrong and I don't have the word to describe it in any language, and for the moment I feel impoverished.

Finally, I come to know that, no matter how many tongues I contort, I will never have all the right words.

About the author

Photo by Emma Dodge Hanson

Samantha Dunn

Samantha Dunn was raised in northern New Mexico and spent years in Australia and France. She is a widely published journalist, contributing to a number of magazines and newspapers in the United States.

The fonts used in this book are from the Garamond family

Made in the USA
San Bernardino, CA
17 March 2015